Meg was in trouble. Big trouble.

When Cruz opened the car door and slid inside, the edges of his dark hair were damp with sweat. He flipped the air on high and turned to face Meg. "We've got a little bit of a situation here," he said.

Meg's stomach clenched. Cruz's voice was soft, not giving anything away. But he couldn't control the emotion in his eyes so well.

"What?"

He put his hand on her arm. "Somebody was in your apartment and they did a real job on it. I want you to stay here until they work the scene."

In her apartment. A real job. She let out a deep breath and sank back into the seat. Cruz dropped his arm, giving Meg the chance she needed to wrench open the door and bolt across the street. He didn't catch her until she was at the steps.

"Meg, damn it," he said. "It's bad."

"I have to know," she said. "Please…"

BEVERLY LONG

SECURE LOCATION

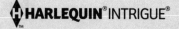

HARLEQUIN® INTRIGUE®

For Lydia: so sweet, so beautiful. You are loved!

Recycling programs for this product may not exist in your area.

ISBN-13: 978-0-373-74739-9

SECURE LOCATION

Copyright © 2013 by Beverly R. Long

Printed in U.S.A.

www.Harlequin.com

ABOUT THE AUTHOR

As a child, Beverly Long used to take a flashlight to bed so that she could hide under the covers and read. Once a teenager, more often than not, the books she chose were romance novels. Now she gets to keep the light on as long as she wants, and there's always a romance novel on her nightstand. With both a bachelor's and a master's degree in business and more than twenty years of experience as a human resources director, she now enjoys the opportunity to write her own stories. She considers her books to be a great success if they compel the reader to stay up way past their bedtime.

Beverly loves to hear from readers. Visit www.beverlylong.com or like her at www.facebook.com/BeverlyLong.Romance.

Books by Beverly Long

HARLEQUIN INTRIGUE
1388—RUNNING FOR HER LIFE
1412—DEADLY FORCE**
1418—SECURE LOCATION**

**The Detectives

CAST OF CHARACTERS

Meg Montoya—A year ago, she walked away from her marriage to Cruz Montoya. Now, her life is threatened. Can she accept Cruz's help and risk that he'll learn the secret that she's hidden for twenty years?

Cruz Montoya—He vows to protect his ex-wife, even though she's made it clear that she doesn't need it. He loves her. Always has, always will. After one reckless night of passion, Cruz realizes the stakes have suddenly gotten much higher. Can he protect the woman he loves—and their child?

Scott Slater—He's Meg's boss but does he want to be more? Is that what prompts him to suggest to the police that Cruz is responsible for Meg's troubles? Or is he simply trying to shift the investigation in another direction?

Charlotte Anderson—She's a super-efficient assistant who claims to support Meg, but does she really? Is it possible that she's jealous of Meg, who seems to have everything while Charlotte has nothing?

Oscar Warren—He's an ex-con that Meg has gone out of her way to assist. Is he being honest when he says that he likes and respects Meg?

Mason Hawkins—He's got a grudge against the management of the BJM Hotel because they didn't appreciate his talent. Is he angry enough to kill?

Tom Looney—He's hiding a secret life. How far will he go to make sure that his privacy is not jeopardized?

Troy Blakely—He was a short-timer at the hotel but employed long enough for others to see his anger management problem. Is he the type to strike out against a former employer?

Chapter One

Meg was halfway through her salad when her office door swung open. She looked up, saw him, swallowed too quickly and coughed as if she had a two-pack-a-day habit. When she finally stopped, her eyes were tearing.

Cruz hadn't moved from the doorway.

His gaze lingered on her face, bold, blatant. Heat was the immediate reaction, starting in her neck and flooding her cheeks until finally it seemed as if the top of her head might explode. Finally, he shifted his gaze and she let out the breath she'd been holding.

The curtains on the big windows were open and he studied the hotel's towering cypress trees, the manicured flower beds and the exquisite stonework. He gave no indication that he was impressed by the lushness of the San Antonio River Walk. Turning ever so slightly, he inspected the room, looking at the cherry desk, the matching credenza, the leather chairs. "Nice digs," he said finally.

Her first corner office. She'd worked twelve-hour days for the past year to earn it. "It's fine," she said, ignoring the impulse to defend the space.

He nonchalantly rubbed his hand across his chin. Her mostly empty stomach jumped when she saw that he wasn't wearing a ring. It was pure craziness that she wasn't sure if that made her sad or happy. She didn't want him to be alone. Had never wanted that. But then again, she couldn't stand the thought of him being with someone else.

Which was why she tried not to think of him at all. And most days, she managed pretty well. Leaving him had almost killed her. She couldn't risk that kind of pain again. "Look," she said, "I don't mean to be rude but I'm pretty busy."

He tilted his chin down. He needed a shave. "It's been a year, Meg, and you don't have ten minutes?"

It had been one year and twenty-two days. She'd seen him only once during that time period, but he'd been unconscious, probably hadn't even known she was there. "I'm sorry. You caught me a little off guard."

He nodded and continued to boldly stare at her. Her bare arms felt chilled and she resisted the urge to pull at the edges of her V-neck blouse.

She stood up fast. So fast that her skirt caught

the corner of the plastic container on her desk and flipped it. Salad spilled out onto the desk.

She ignored it. There'd be plenty of time to clean up the mess later. When he was gone.

"I like the hair," he said, surprising her.

She wore it shorter than she had before. "Yours is longer," she said. He'd worn a buzz cut for years and while his thick dark hair was still cut close, it was long enough for anyone to see the natural wave. Other than that, he looked the same.

She thought she recognized the faded brown cargo shorts and the T-shirt that was stretched across his broad chest. She definitely knew the well-worn sandals.

He looked at the nameplate on her desk. "Senior Vice President, huh? Congratulations."

It was her turn to nod. He'd never been a jerk about her working. Maybe because he'd been raised by a woman who had worked way too hard. "How's your mom?" she asked.

"Good. Still at the hotel but she's finally cut back to part-time."

Maria Montoya had been the hardest working, most welcoming woman that she'd ever met. Her husband had left her and their four children when Cruz, the oldest, was just twelve. She'd managed to hold her family together, to feed and clothe them working six days a week cleaning rooms at a hotel. When Meg had told her goodbye, it was the first time she'd seen disapproval in her soft brown eyes.

"And Sam?" Without thought, her eyes went to Cruz's leg. It had been shattered by a bullet when Cruz and Sam had tried to stop a robbery-in-progress at a small coffeehouse. Sam wasn't blood but the closest thing to it. He'd been Cruz's partner for five years and he'd been the one at the scene, urging Cruz to hang on. Had been the one to call her, to tell her the awful news.

"Claire's pregnant. They just found out."

Meg leaned back against her desk, letting the wood take her weight. "That's great," she said, hearing the brittleness in her voice, hoping like hell that she was hiding it.

He moved farther into the room. Close enough that she could smell his scent—it was soap and citrus and evoked memories of warm summer nights and a porch swing that took up half the patio. Knowing that he'd always been too good at simply looking at her and knowing what she was thinking, she moved behind her desk and turned to the window.

The River Walk was coming to life. By early evening, the stone walkways would be filled with tourists. Music would pour out of buildings. Lovers would stroll in the moonlight, hand in hand, their faces close.

She always pulled the drapes at night. It was easier. "I'll send them a card," she murmured.

"You do that." He stared at her. "But don't you have bigger things to worry about?"

Damn. It was what she'd been afraid of since she'd seen him standing in the doorway. "I'm not sure I know what you're talking about?" she hedged.

"Oh, I think you do. I got a telephone call yesterday from the San Antonio Police Department. They were interested in what I'd been doing for the last couple of weeks. Once I convinced them that I'd been working my ass off in Chicago, they were a little more forthcoming. Professional courtesy and all."

She turned and faced him. "I didn't send them looking for you. I didn't even tell them about you."

"That became abundantly clear when I talked with them. And you know what?" he asked, his voice louder now. "That's what really got to me. Don't you think I'd want to know that my wife was getting death threats?"

"*Ex-wife,* Cruz."

"I read the fine print," he replied, his tone full of sarcasm. "What the hell is going on, Meg?"

She wished she knew. "It's nothing. A few threats, that's all."

"Detective Myers said your boss told them you had an ex-husband who might have a reason to be pissed off."

"I never suggested that and I certainly didn't ask Scott to say anything. I guess he's…he's more worried than I thought."

"Of course," Cruz said, his tone mocking.

She understood. After all, she'd deliberately let Cruz believe the worst, that she'd followed Scott to San Antonio because they were more than colleagues. She'd had no choice. She wasn't going to tell him the truth. Ever. "Did the police ask you to come here?"

"No. I did let Detective Myers know that I was coming. Professional—"

"Courtesy," she finished. "I got it. Well, your timing is bad. I was just on my way out."

He looked at the pile of salad on her desk. "Really?"

"Shopping," she said. He hated to shop.

Grabbing her suit jacket off the back of her chair, she stuffed her arms through the sleeves. It was a hundred in the shade but she didn't care. She needed armor. Once she was safely in the car, away from him, she'd yank it off, crank up the air-conditioning, blast the Boss on her CD player and forget about it all.

With deliberate strides, she walked past him. She offered up a prayer to the office gods that Charlotte was still at lunch. She didn't want to have to make introductions.

The executive offices flanked the lobby on the left and right sides. VPs of Finance and Purchasing next to her; Guest Services and Facilities on the other side. All of them reported to Scott, who claimed a corner of the third floor as his own.

Her heels echoed softly on the slate floor as she walked down the side hallway. He followed, a half step behind. She wondered if that was deliberate. Did he limp? Was he trying to hide it from her? She couldn't look without making it obvious.

A sharp right would take her past the guest elevators and concierge. She veered left, heading straight for the service elevator that would take her to the parking garage.

The elevator was empty. She got in and he followed. He stood close to her, as if it was okay to breach her personal space. She edged away, until her back hit the wall. Then she had to reach past him to punch *B*.

"Where do you park?" he asked.

"Where all employees park. In the lower level lot."

He didn't answer. When the door opened, he moved fast. He held up a hand, stopping her.

"Oh, good grief. It's very safe," she said. "There are security cameras everywhere."

He rolled his eyes. "And if this is like most parking lots, there's nobody actually watching them. So all the good they'll do is maybe, if you're really lucky, they'll catch your attacker on tape. Excellent evidence and all but if you're already dead, it's not going to be that much help to you."

She didn't bother to answer. Instead, she pointed to the far left side. "After you," she said.

He didn't limp. Not even a little. She felt insanely glad for him. He'd always been an athlete. If he hadn't been riding his bike or running along the lake, he'd been catching a quick pickup basketball game with whoever happened to be at the courts. "Congrats on the rehab," she said. "You must have been pretty diligent."

He stopped but didn't turn around. "I had a lot of time on my hands," he said, his delivery stiff.

After you left, she added silently.

She didn't need his contempt. She had plenty of her own. When he started walking again, she let him get a little farther ahead. Even so, when he stopped very suddenly, she almost rammed into him.

"Wha—" The words caught in her throat as he

grabbed her arm, yanked her behind one of the stone pillars that supported the roof, and pressed her body against the cold, rough concrete.

She could feel his back against her back.

She twisted her neck to look. Cruz had pulled his gun and his arm was raised, level with his shoulder. He rotated in a half circle. Then, with his free hand, he pressed against her side, to shift her. In tandem, they sidestepped halfway around the pillar. Once he'd done a three-sixty inspection of the garage, he lowered his arm and moved away.

"You okay?" he asked.

What the heck? She was about to demand an explanation when he pointed in the direction of her car.

The front and back windows on her red Toyota were smashed and it looked as if someone had taken a baseball bat to the hood. On the rear bumper, *BITCH* was sprayed in white paint. The passenger-side window, which was facing them, had been almost completely knocked out, just a few shards of glass remained.

Her heart, already racing in her chest, kicked up another notch.

"You're close enough," he said.

Like hell. She started walking. He didn't try to

hold her back, just fell in step next to her. "Don't touch anything," he said.

As they got closer, a raw and disgusting smell made her gag. They peered inside. Two dead fish, already deteriorating, had been tossed onto the driver's seat. Cruz turned his head. There was violence in his eyes that would have scared her if she hadn't known him so well. And for just a minute, she thought he was going to yell at her, perhaps throw her casual remark about how safe the garage was in her face.

Instead, he said, "I'm going to assume that wasn't the rest of your lunch?"

In spite of it all, she wanted to smile. She'd missed his wicked sense of humor. No one would ever make her laugh the way he had. "I prefer my fish frozen and shrink-wrapped."

"Good plan." He straightened up, pulled a cell phone from his shirt pocket, and handed it to her. "Call the police and your security department, too. Let's hope the camera wasn't broke today."

When she didn't protest, didn't make any noises about him not being the boss of her, Cruz figured she was as shook as she looked. After he'd seen the damage and the dead fish, he'd been this close to losing it but then he'd seen her pale face and her pinched lips and figured she didn't need him to be an ass.

She was too thin. She'd always been in good shape, had worked out regularly, eaten right. But she'd lost at least ten pounds off her frame. She seemed almost fragile. Shiny dark hair with hazel eyes, flawless skin, she still looked very much like the girl next door, even at age thirty-five. He suspected at fifty she'd still be beautiful. At seventy, she'd be lovely. At ninety, she'd be radiant.

He had thought he would see all those ages with her. But then suddenly a year ago, after six years of marriage, she'd kicked him to the curb. And followed her boss to San Antonio.

Wasn't he some kind of stupid fool for thinking more than once in the past year, that just maybe she'd find her way back to Chicago, back to him? But people didn't come back. They moved on. His father had. Moved out and moved on. Started a new family and never came back to his old family. Even though they'd desperately needed him.

His mom had been a rock even though he'd done his very best to make her life miserable. He'd been angry and defiant, determined to prove to everybody that his dad was justified in leaving. But somehow his mother had held her small family together, even when there were weeks where the only food to eat were peanut butter sandwiches.

People managed.

Just like Meg and Slater could manage this.

Scott Slater ran this fancy hotel. He had the money to beef-up security, get some around-the-clock protection.

It wasn't Cruz's problem. And clearly, Meg wasn't overjoyed to see him.

But, he realized, as he walked around the car, each circle making his stomach grip tighter, none of that mattered. He wasn't going anywhere. Not if there was a chance that Meg was in danger.

The creep had been thorough. There was hardly a spot that hadn't been damaged. Somebody had wanted to make a point.

"So who have you pissed off lately?" he asked, without looking at her.

"I don't know. I've been through it a hundred times in my head and I can't think of anybody. The police asked for a list of people that the hotel had terminated in the last year."

It was a good place to start. When people lost jobs, they wanted somebody to blame. The Senior Vice President of Operations was as good as anybody. He'd seen stranger things in his fifteen years on the force. Hell, once a man was stalked for three weeks and ultimately killed because he'd taken somebody's seat on the train. People were squirrelly.

Beat cops arrived before the in-house security, which didn't give him a whole lot of confidence in the hotel staff. He and Meg told their story, everybody walked around the car a couple times, and a whole lot of pictures got taken. Security arrived five minutes later, trailed by Detective Harold Myers. The man was twenty pounds overweight, in his fifties, smelled like cigarettes, and his nose was too big for his face.

They told their story a second time, did some more walk-arounds, and then it was up to the main office to take a look at the security cameras. Cruz managed to keep his I-told-you-so to himself when it became clear that the location of Meg's parking space was about fifteen feet beyond the scope of the camera. But he did want to kick her boss's ass. How could the guy have allowed her to park somewhere where there wasn't even a security camera after she'd received death threats?

But Slater was playing golf and Sanjoi Saketa, the skinny Asian from in-house security, didn't seem inclined to page him. It gave Cruz only a little satisfaction that Meg wasn't demanding that he do so.

Cruz drummed his fingers on the metal desk. "You do have a camera on the entrance and exit, right?"

"Of course," Sanjoi said, sounding a little offended. "There's one gate in and one out. The camera swivels between them, every four seconds."

"Do employees have to swipe a badge to activate the gates?" Cruz asked.

Sanjoi shook his head. "No. Guests park here, as well. The gates are activated by a car pulling up."

Myers shrugged. "It's not the best system, but then again, I've worked this beat for a lot of years and this hotel has had very few problems. Let's take a look at the tapes and try to isolate cars that enter and leave again quickly."

"Is there a camera over the employee entrance?" Cruz asked.

Sanjoi nodded.

"Good. Can you produce a list of every employee who entered the building after Meg did this morning?"

Myers stepped forward. "The list should be given to me," he instructed. "Detective Montoya is not here in an official capacity."

Yeah. He was just the idiot ex-husband. "Let's get out of here," he said to Meg.

"It's not even three o'clock. I can't just leave."

"I thought you were going shopping?"

She was saved from having to answer because at that moment her boss breezed into the office. Cruz could have picked the man out of a lineup in dim lighting. The man's blond hair was always perfectly combed and his six-hundred-dollar suits perfectly pressed. Hell, his golf pants had creases.

The man had been Meg's coworker in Chicago and when he'd accepted a promotion to San Antonio eighteen months ago, Cruz had been happy to see him go. He'd always thought the man was a little too friendly with his wife, although there had never been any reason to think that Meg reciprocated in any way.

He'd felt pretty damn stupid when Meg had followed him here six months later, leaving the same day she'd signed the divorce papers.

Slater ignored him, eyes only for Meg. "Are you all right? This is getting out of control."

You think? Cruz put a proprietary hand on the small of Meg's back and enjoyed seeing the tightening of Slater's chin before the man put his game face back on.

"It's been a while, Cruz."

The man made friendly and extended his hand. Cruz ignored it. He pressed on Meg's side with two fingers. "We should go."

"It's the middle of the afternoon," she said, shaking her head. She moved a few inches away from him.

"And your car is trashed in the middle of a public parking lot. Give yourself a break. You're going to need to contact your insurance company, get started on a rental."

Her shoulders sagged. He hated seeing that.

Still, he could tell by the way she was chewing on the corner of her mouth that she wanted to be the good soldier and finish out her shift.

But then, common sense, nerves, fatigue, whatever, finally won. She looked at Mr. Perfect. "I'll be in early tomorrow," she promised.

They walked in silence to Cruz's white Ford rental car. Once inside, he couldn't help himself. "I think he's gotten shorter. And he might want to cut back on the Botox. Half his face didn't move." It was a cheap shot. The guy looked good. Polished. Smooth. Everything that Cruz wasn't.

She rolled her eyes. "Just drive. Please."

Other than *turn here, turn there,* it was the last thing she said to him for twenty minutes. Finally, she pointed to a group of three-story brick buildings that all looked the same. "My condo is in the middle building."

Decent neighborhood. Not much character. Certainly not what he'd expected. "I figured Slater was the downtown loft type."

She gave him a look that could kill. "I live alone."

Cruz, who was rarely surprised, had to work real hard not to show that she managed to shock him. She'd followed the man halfway across the country. To live alone? Was it as simple as the two executives felt the need to be very discreet? Would there have been push-back from the corporate office if their relationship became known? He had a hundred questions.

But he didn't ask. Didn't want to admit how much he wanted to know. Had been a cop too long to show his hand.

The neighborhood was quiet. Just one old lady hauling a shopping cart behind her. Still, he went two more blocks and then turned around and came at it from the opposite direction. Nothing jumped out at him. There were a few parked cars along the road, all empty. He pulled into the lot, parked and turned to her. "Give me your keys," he said.

She scowled at him. "Don't tell me what to do."

Okay. This was good. She'd evidently spent the drive regrouping. But what the hell did she expect? He was a cop. Her car had just been vandalized and now he wanted to check her apartment. He took a deep breath. "If you could be so kind as to give me your keys, I would be grateful for the opportunity to enter in advance of you in an effort to survey your living quarters and ensure that it remains an environment conducive to your ongoing safety. But only if it's no trouble, of course."

She let out an audible sigh. "Let's just get this over with."

How could he have forgotten? She liked ending things. Quickly. "I guess I made an assumption that sleeping with you for six years entitled me to a little familiarity."

Pink blotches suddenly appeared on her fair skin, just above the collar of her gray blouse, proving that some things never did change. When Meg was frustrated or angry, she didn't hide it well. They used to joke about it, saying that she'd make a lousy undercover detective.

Was she remembering all the times they'd been more than a *little* familiar? How they made love in the park, with oblivious strangers just feet away? Or perhaps the weekend they moved into their house? Eighteen hours. Every damn room. "Meg?" he said, his voice cracking.

She shook her head. "Just forget it. Please. Go do your thing. All I want is to be able to go inside my house and forget about the last three hours." She tossed the keys in his lap. "Unit Six. The number is next to the door."

He pointed at the car keys in the ignition. "It's too hot to sit out here without the air on. Keep the car running. If you see or hear anything that looks weird, get the hell out of here. Call 911 on the way."

She reached out a hand but pulled back before she touched him. "Cruz...be careful, okay?"

He nodded, not trusting his own voice. It was the same thing she'd said to him every morning for six years. Of course, the morning he'd been shot, she'd already been gone for six months.

When he'd woken up in the hospital hours later and she'd been there, the damn pain in his leg had suddenly seemed worth it. She was back.

And then she'd left again. And no amount of pain medication had been able to take that hurt away.

"Yeah, right," he said. He closed the car door softly and walked toward her condo. When he got to her door, it looked like all the other doors. Almost.

It was ajar. Just inches. But enough that when he looked inside and saw the damage, he knew the truth.

Meg was in trouble. Big trouble.

Chapter Two

When Cruz opened the car door and slid inside, the edges of his dark hair were damp with sweat. He flipped the air on high, and turned to face Meg. "We've got a little bit of a situation here," he said.

Meg's stomach clenched. Cruz's voice was soft, not giving anything away. But he wasn't able to control the emotion in his eyes, as well. He was pissed.

"What?"

He put his hand on her arm. "Somebody was in your condo and they did a real job on it. I called Myers and he and his people are on the way. I want you to stay here until they work the scene."

In her condo. A real job. She let out a deep breath and sank back into the seat. Cruz dropped his arm, giving Meg the chance she needed to wrench open the door and bolt across the street. He didn't catch her until she was at the steps.

"Meg, damn it," he said. "It's bad."

"I have to know," she said. "Please."

He ran a hand through his hair. "Okay. But please don't touch anything."

The cupboard doors were open but the shelves were empty, save one lone cup that was so far back that it had escaped attention. Shards of new blue Crate and Barrel plates strewn from one end of the ceramic countertop to the other made a crazy kind of confetti when mixed with the remnants of the sturdy brown stoneware that she'd had since college. The refrigerator door was also open, wrenched so hard that it now hung crookedly. On the top shelf, a plastic pitcher lay on its side, the orange juice pooled around it, contained by the upturned edge of the shelf. The eggs she'd bought two days ago had been thrown at the stove and yolk and shell and slimy egg white had dried on the black front.

On the small table that separated her kitchen from the living room, the plant had been upturned, sending potting soil flying. What she could see of the living room didn't encourage her to look further. The cushions were still on the couch but each had a haphazard slice in the fabric. The entertainment center had been pushed over and the television was facedown on the carpet. It looked as if someone had hacked the back of it with an ax.

"I...I've been...wanting a flat screen," she said.

She forced a smile at Cruz and knew she'd failed when his mouth tightened even more.

"Well, then," he said. He paused. "It's gonna be okay, Meg. I promise."

Her chest felt tight and it was hard to breathe. What if she'd been home? What if she'd been sleeping and had awakened to find this kind of madness looming over her?

Would she be dead?

Cruz stepped in front of her, maybe to get her attention, maybe just to block the room. "And you still have no idea who might do this?" he asked.

"Of course not," she said. This was so destructive, maybe even hateful. No one hated her.

Did they? Someone had, but it had been years ago. Twenty, in fact. Margaret Mae Gunderson had let everyone down. And there had been hate.

But how could anyone believe that the price she'd paid had not been dear enough?

A car door slammed. Then two more in quick succession. Cruz was already at the front door. "Myers and his team."

It took them over two hours to work their way through the mess. Meg followed them from the living room back to the bedrooms. The spare room, which served as her office, had the least damage. The carpet was wet and her books sat in a sodden pile in the middle. The bucket the intruder had used to carry water had been tossed in the corner.

"Your bucket?" Detective Myers asked.

"Yes. From under my kitchen sink."

"Tag it and bag it," he said to the female officer.

The damage in her bedroom was much worse. Her clothes had been pulled from both her closet and drawers and sprayed with the horrible red paint. The bedcovers had been pulled off and her mattress had been sliced multiple times. The mirror above her dresser was cracked.

When she entered the bathroom, the smell almost knocked her back. Perfume bottles had been smashed in the sink. On top of the shards of glass lay more rotted fish. The mirror was cracked and across it, written in red paint, was *BITCH*.

Her knees felt weak and her vision narrowed.

Cruz grabbed her elbow and pulled her back. "She's seen enough," he said, looking over his shoulder at Detective Myers. He gently prodded her back to the kitchen and sat her down on the chair. "Put your head between your knees," he said.

She waved him away. "I'm fine. I just need a minute."

Detective Myers gave her three minutes before he followed her. "It's probably hard to tell but do you know if anything is missing?" he asked.

"I…" She licked her lips and wished she had water. "I don't think so."

The man nodded. "To do this kind of damage, the intruder was here for a while. Maybe one of the neighbors saw something. My team will canvas the area. We'll check the street cameras, too, and maybe we'll get lucky there."

"Thank you," she said. He seemed like a good cop. Straightforward. She was going to have to tell him everything. Just in case. But not with Cruz standing there. Not with him in the same town. Even if Detective Myers swore to keep her secret, she knew Cruz's ability to compel even the most reluctant of witnesses to speak up. Could she gamble that he wouldn't prod and needle Detective Myers until the man surrendered the information?

"We dusted everything for prints," Detective Myers said. "I'll need yours and whoever else has been in your apartment for the last several months to rule them out."

"I'll get you the names," she said. She'd had Charlotte and her mother over for dinner a month ago. That was it.

Detective Myers turned his attention toward Cruz. "I suppose you can account for your whereabouts since seven this morning?"

Cruz pulled his travel itinerary out of his shorts pocket and handed it to the older man. "Arrived at the airport, rented a car, drove I-95 to the River Walk. No stops in between."

Detective Myers nodded, tucked the itinerary into his notebook, and put his pen in his shirt pocket. Meg had no doubt the guy was going to check it out, maybe look at a few more street cameras along Cruz's route. "I'll be in touch," the man said to Meg. "I'll let you know when you can start cleaning this up. Where will you be staying until then?"

"I…uh…guess I'll stay at the hotel. In the summer we're not as full as usual so that shouldn't be a problem."

The detective turned toward Cruz. "And what about you, Mr. Montoya?"

He needed to point the nose of his rental car toward Chicago and not stop until he ran into Lake Michigan.

"I'll be at the hotel, too," he said.

Meg whipped her head in his direction. "That's not necessary," she said.

He waved away her argument, clearly not wanting to discuss it in front of Detective Myers. The older man looked at Cruz, then at her, speculation in his eyes. Evidently not seeing too much that disturbed him, he motioned for them to leave. "We'll finish up here. I'll be in touch."

When they were back in the car, the seat was

so hot that it burned skin. Meg tucked her skirt under her legs and gingerly reached for the metal clasp of her seat belt.

Cruz started the car and cranked up the air-conditioning. He didn't pull out. Just sat in the driver's seat, looking forward. Finally he turned toward her.

"Your car. This. You know I had nothing to do with it, right?" His voice cracked at the end.

She stared at him and wanted to tell him that of all the people in the world, he was the person she trusted the most.

Instead, she turned and faced out the window. Two beat cops were stringing up yellow crime scene tape across her door. "Of course not. I mean, it's been a year," she added, still staring at her condo. "And it's not like our divorce was a nasty one."

No. It had been very civilized. Probably because she'd insisted the two of them only communicate through their respective attorneys. Once the house had been sold, they'd split the proceeds and that had been the end of it. Very, very civilized. A perfect divorce, really.

"Look," she said, turning partway back but not quite enough to meet his eyes. "It's nice of you to offer to stay for a few days. But I'm sure it's hard to get the time off. I'll be fine, really. I just need to be a little more careful until they catch the person responsible for this."

"I'm staying," he said.

"No."

He shook his head. "Last time I checked, you weren't in charge of who gets to vacation in Texas."

She pressed her lips together. "Don't be ridiculous."

"I'm looking forward to visiting Elsa and her family. They built a new house about forty miles north of San Antonio."

"They finally did it, huh?" she asked before she could think better of it. His sister Elsa had been the sister that Meg had never had. And always wanted. Her husband had been transferred from Chicago to Texas a few years after Meg and Cruz had married. "You know, I thought about calling your sister after I moved here. But I wasn't sure anybody in your family wanted to hear from me," she admitted.

Cruz shrugged. "The two of you were friends. Just because we're no longer married, that doesn't have to change."

He was wrong. Everything changed when you got divorced. Family banded together and friends had to pick sides. At least she hadn't stayed in the same town. Their friends hadn't had to choose whether it would be him or her that got invited to the next dinner party.

She wondered how many invitations he'd accepted. He was too good-looking, too nice, to be alone for long.

"Really, Cruz," she said, her voice sounding loud in the small car. "I insist. It's too much for me to ask. You should go home."

"I'm staying," he repeated.

He's staying. Part of her wanted to get down and kiss the hard, sunbaked ground. Cruz was a good cop. Even when he'd been young and fresh out of the academy and his friends were still idiots on Friday nights, he'd taken his responsibilities to serve and protect seriously.

Don't you dare lie to me. His buddies on the force used to tease him after a few beers. It was well-known that whenever Cruz interrogated a witness or a suspect and hissed those words, that he was dead serious. The man hated being lied to. And given that her entire life was one big lie, she was the absolute worst person for him to fall in love with.

She'd loved him since their third date. He'd taken her to Wrigley Field, bought her hot dogs and cold beer, and broken the third finger on his left hand protecting her face from a fly ball. They spent an hour in the emergency room and another twelve in his bed. She'd married him that Christmas and six years later they were still on the road to happily ever after. She'd actually begun to believe that her past didn't matter, that maybe it was possible to put it all behind her.

He didn't want children. She'd assumed it had something to do with growing up poor and having had the responsibility of helping raise his younger brothers and sisters. He told her on their second date that he'd changed all the dirty diapers he intended to ever change. No procreation for him.

It was perfect. And it stayed that way for a long time.

Then his brother's wife had gotten pregnant. Then his sister. Another sister-in-law. It was an avalanche of babies. And he'd suddenly started hinting around that maybe it wouldn't be so bad if they had a little Montoya of their own.

She'd had no alternative but to leave. She couldn't tell him the truth. She'd spent a lifetime weaving a series of lies so tight that no one would have ever guessed the havoc she'd wreaked. It had been a wide path of destruction. Broken marriages, families fleeing their houses in the dark of the night and a thing so horrible she never said the words out loud.

If he knew the truth, he'd have never trusted her with any child and definitely not his child.

"What are you going to do about clothes?" he

asked, whipping her back to the present. "I don't think there was much in your closet that wasn't sprayed with paint."

"I guess it's a good thing I've got some suits at the dry cleaners. I keep an extra pair of shoes at work, too. I can pick up the rest of what I'll need in the short-term."

"You're being pretty calm about this," he said.

She wasn't calm. She felt exposed and dirty and it was a terrible thing to believe that somebody wanted to deliberately hurt her. When the threats had started, she'd been shaken. Who wouldn't have been? She'd picked up her voice mail only to hear some distorted voice ramble on about killing her. Then she'd gotten a letter in the mail. Words cut out of a magazine and pasted on a page, just like in the movies. The message had been short but not sweet. *You need to pay for what you did.*

She'd wanted to tear up the letter and pretend that it had never come. But Charlotte had seen the mail—there was no going backward. Meg had shown Scott the letter and told him about the telephone message. Together, they'd called the police. When Detective Myers probed about possible suspects, she'd told him the truth. She had no idea.

She'd never suspected Cruz. Certainly hadn't given Scott any reason to think that Cruz could be involved. But now he was caught up in it.

He deserved better. He'd always deserved better than her. The only solution was to get him to leave San Antonio.

"I need to see Scott," she said, as he pulled the rental car into a stall in the parking deck. She could see the tightening of his jaw muscles.

"Do whatever you need to do," he said, his voice stiff. "I'm going to get a room."

She put a hand out, grabbing his bare arm. His skin was cold from the blasting air-conditioning and the muscles in his forearms were tight. It brought back sudden memories of cool naked skin and him balanced over her, weight on his arms, just before he took her.

She jerked her hand away. "Our rooms are really expensive," she warned, her voice cracking.

He raised his eyebrows. "You think I couldn't tell that from the lobby? I can afford it, Meg. I haven't had much else to spend my money on this last year."

She'd hurt him badly. It made her ache. "Well, you shouldn't spend what you have here. Detective Myers seems very capable." She got out of the car, shut the door hard, and quickly walked toward the garage elevator. He caught up with her in just a few strides.

"Why the hell don't you want me here?" he demanded.

She whirled on him. "I hurt you, Cruz. I know

that. And for what it's worth, I'm sorry. But we both need to move on. And neither one of us can do that if you're here."

She could see the rapid beat of his heart in the hollow of his neck. "I won't leave knowing that you're in danger. I'm a good cop, Meg. I can help Myers. Let me start with the list of people who've been fired from this hotel in the last year."

"That's confidential information."

"I don't care. You've got an in with the boss," he said, his voice getting loud. "He's got the authority to give me the names. Ask him. Or I will."

She let out a big huff of breath. Then she raised her index finger and pointed toward the lobby. "Fine."

"I'm not sure what Myers asked for but I want name, address, phone, emergency contact information, title, dates of employment and reason they were let go. I imagine you've got all that in some database."

They did. She nodded.

"Pictures, too," he said.

"We don't keep that in the human resources system."

"Yeah, but I bet you do in your security system. Every time somebody gets their picture taken for a swipe card, a copy is probably stored in your system."

"I'll have to check. Detective Myers didn't ask for them."

"He should have," Cruz said, shaking his head.

"He seems competent," she said, not knowing exactly why she felt compelled to defend the detective. Maybe because she hadn't been married to him and he didn't have the ability to make her want the things she couldn't have. "I'll talk to Scott about the list."

"Thank you." His voice was softer now. "When you find out what room you're staying in, I want the one next to it. Make sure there are interior connecting doors."

She started to protest but he held up a hand. "It's not going to do me much good if something happens and I'm sixteen floors away."

Meg resisted the urge to scream in frustration and went to find Scott. He was talking on the telephone but he waved her into the room and motioned for her to take a chair.

Scott Slater was a nice man. He worked hard, treated his employees fairly. They'd been peers in Chicago and she'd been genuinely happy for him when he'd gotten the promotion and a chance to run a hotel in San Antonio. When she'd had to suddenly leave Chicago just months later, he'd been a godsend. She'd called and inquired and he'd offered her a job without asking any questions.

In the past year, they'd worked hard to build the infrastructure that it took to keep a six-hundred-room hotel operating smoothly. In the past three months, they'd had dinner a few times. They'd talked about work, mostly.

It had been fine. And wasn't that enough? She'd had a great love. Now what she needed was companionship. Common interests. Strong regard.

Ugh.

Maybe she should get a dog.

Scott hung up the phone. "What's wrong?" he asked.

"My condo was vandalized. Really wrecked, actually." She said it calmly, as if she were reporting on the monthly financials. Nobody needed to know that her insides were churning and every time she closed her eyes she could see the cascade of broken cutlery strewn across the kitchen counter. "I'm going to need a place to stay. I was hoping I could have a room here."

He stood up and came around the front of the desk. He stood close. "Of course. I'll give you one of the executive suites. But, Meg, this is getting ridiculous. First your car, then your apartment. What do the police think?"

"They don't know what to think."

"I'm worried about you," he said. "You know that…I care about you."

She did. On their last date, two months ago, they'd gone to one of the new Japanese restaurants. When he'd taken her home and tried to kiss her, she'd tensed up like a board. Embarrassed, she'd mumbled something about needing more time and he'd backed off.

They hadn't been out again and Scott had never mentioned it. When they were in public, he was always absolutely appropriate. But when they were alone, his glances lingered, his smile was more intimate.

He was being a gentleman, biding his time.

It made her feel even worse that she'd let him be the fall guy when she'd needed an excuse to leave Cruz. During their marriage, Cruz had mentioned a couple times that he thought Scott was interested in more than her work ethic. So he'd readily believed her when she'd told him that Scott had asked her to be with him in San Antonio. Had let Cruz believe the worst.

She was going to be walking a tightrope with both of them in the same city.

"I mentioned Cruz to the police," Scott admitted. "I know you were adamant that he couldn't have had anything to do with the threats but I couldn't be as sure."

"I understand. It's okay. He thinks he might be

able to help. He'd like the room next to mine. Just in case, you know."

Scott drummed his fingers on the desk. "Well, now I'm a little sorry I offered up his name."

She nodded. That made two of them. "He'll be here a few days at the most," she said.

Scott picked up his phone and arranged for Meg's and Cruz's rooms. "Is there anything else I can do for you?" he asked.

"Can I share the list of terminated employees with Cruz?"

Scott nodded. "Give him whatever you think will be helpful. I want this to be over. And I want him back in Chicago," he added wryly.

"Me, too," she said. She turned and walked out of the office. Cruz Montoya had been the first man she'd loved. She suspected he would be the only man she'd ever love. And Scott deserved better than that. Once this craziness was over and Cruz was back in Chicago, she was going to tell him so. Maybe it would mean the end of their working relationship. If so, she'd have to deal with that.

As she walked down the hallway, she pulled her cell phone out of her purse. She was surprised when Charlotte picked up.

"Hey, what are you still doing there?" Meg asked. "I was going to leave a message for tomorrow."

"Just finishing up some things. I checked your

speech for tomorrow night, made sure the changes were there. Then I ran the financials that you'll need next week."

Meg was insanely glad to be talking about work. Where she felt in control. Competent. Energized.

Or she used to, anyway. Someone was intent upon spoiling the salvation she'd clung to for the past year.

"Thank you so much," she said. Charlotte was amazing. If Meg worked a twelve-hour day, Charlotte stayed for thirteen. "Well, go home soon," Meg ordered lightly. "Your mom will be worried."

"I promise. She won't call you again."

"You know I didn't think anything of that," Meg said. "She's sweet."

"Maybe," Charlotte said, her tone noncommittal. "That's what I get for letting her move in. Anyway, what's with the salad on the desk?"

Meg had forgotten about that. "I'll get it in the morning," she said.

"Already done," Charlotte assured her. "Everything okay? I heard about your car."

That hit a nerve. She hated it when people talked about her. "From?"

"Sanjoi in Security. I think he figured I knew."

She said it casually but Meg caught the inference. *I should have known.*

Charlotte liked to be in the know. And in control. The woman was practically a machine when it came to running the office—details didn't get missed, appointments didn't get forgotten, reports were never late. Well, sometimes she did forget to tell Meg that Scott had called but the woman handled a frightening amount of work with relative ease.

"Do the police think it has anything to do with that letter you received?" Charlotte asked.

"Perhaps. They're investigating. In fact, that's why I'm calling. Can you run me a report? I need…"

Meg gave her the details, including the need for pictures from the security system. Charlotte assured her that she'd get the information right away and put it on Meg's desk.

Meg ended the conversation without telling Charlotte that she was staying at the hotel, with her ex-husband a mere doorway away. She'd have to tell her eventually but after the day she'd had, she just didn't have the strength to stand up to Charlotte's inevitable questions.

She took the elevator back to the lobby, turned the corner and saw Cruz standing to the left of the gleaming wood and marble registration counter, feet spread hip-distance apart, arms crossed over his chest. Six feet of hard muscle and grim determination watching everybody and everything that was going on. His medium-sized duffel bag was sitting next to him. She suspected it was filled with more T-shirts and cargo shorts.

"Everything settled?" he asked.

"Yes. I'll get your room key and you can get unpacked. If you're hungry, the restaurant in the hotel has pretty good food or there are all kinds of places along the River Walk."

He studied her. "What are your plans?"

"Well, I guess my first stop is the dry cleaner. I want to get there before they close. Then I'll swing by my office, do some work for a while, and pick up the list you requested. I'll slide it under your door."

"I'm going with you," he said. "Dry cleaner, then dinner. Together."

Didn't he understand? She couldn't allow herself the luxury of slipping back, even an inch, into the past—to when things had been easy between the two of them. "I don't think so," she said.

"Come on, Meg. Cut me some slack. And yourself, too. I've been traveling since early morning. I missed lunch and you didn't eat much of your salad. Can't we just run the errands and have dinner? Can we keep this simple just for tonight?"

She wanted to say no. But what he said made sense. And she didn't want to stand in the lobby arguing about it. A couple of the registration representatives were already craning their necks, hoping to get a better view. The grapevine was alive and blooming and the story would grow exponentially by morning, until the truth was unrecognizable. *Meg Montoya had a fight with a guest. She pushed him, he fell backward, hit his head and now the hotel is getting sued.* Or some version of that.

"Oh, fine. But don't expect me to give in this easy every time."

Chapter Three

Outside Meg's room, Cruz took her key card and unlocked the door. He pushed it open with his foot and scanned the room. Larger than he expected but then again, it appeared she was a big deal. *Sr. Vice President.* She'd been a director in Chicago.

Obviously, Slater had offered more than just a warm bed.

The room had blond wood floors, lots of blues and greens, and a king-size bed. One step down there was a sitting area with a couch and a big flat-screen television. The sliding glass door at the far end was closed but the vertical blinds had been tilted just enough to let the late-afternoon sunshine spill in and dance across the glossy floor. He glanced into the bathroom. Big shower, plenty of towels and one of those stupid sinks that sat *on* the counter.

He hadn't been in a room this nice since…hell, since he and Meg had celebrated their fifth wedding anniversary on Mackinaw Island in Michigan. They'd made the reservation at the Grand Hotel and had joked that this time, they would manage to see the island, something they hadn't accomplished on their honeymoon when their focus had been on indoor activities.

They'd been wrong. The bike shorts had never even come out of the suitcase. And most of the meals had been delivered by room service. Cruz had gone back to work a very happy man.

He'd never dreamed that it would all fall apart a year later. He looked at Meg, wondering if she was remembering. But her face was blank and she was looking at her watch.

He crossed the room, checked to make sure the slider had a safety bar at the bottom, and then stepped toward the door that connected the two rooms. He flipped the bolt. "Keep this unlocked," he said. She nodded, still clearly not happy that he was staying.

Tough. She'd probably be unhappier if she were dead.

He didn't intend to let the son of a bitch who'd trashed her car and apartment anywhere near her. He might not have Slater's ability to kiss corporate ass but he was good at his job. Really good. He would keep her safe. And he would make sure that the person responsible for terrorizing her and putting the fear into her eyes was strung up and left swinging in the wind.

His room was an exact duplicate of hers. He took just a minute to crank up the air-conditioning and grab a clean T-shirt from his bag. He stepped into the bathroom, splashed water on his face, shucked off one shirt and pulled on another. All the while, he listened for the door. He wasn't concerned about someone trying to get in but he thought she might make a break for it.

But when he walked through the connecting door, she was still standing in the middle of the room. "Really, Cruz," she said. "This isn't necessary. It's just down the street. You should unpack, get some rest."

He didn't bother to answer—just motioned for her to follow him. They walked down the short hallway to the elevators in silence. Ten floors down, they exited the hotel at street level, on the other side of the River Walk. It was a different world. There were no lush walkways or meandering tourists. The sidewalk was a mile of white cement and the trees along it offered little shade from the late-afternoon sun that was still mercilessly hot. Buses rumbled by, belching exhaust, picking up locals, delivering them either to or from work.

Cruz fell into step next to Meg. He looked

around but nobody seemed to be paying any attention to them.

The dry cleaner was a small Asian woman who greeted Meg warmly and looked at him with unguarded speculation. Meg didn't introduce him. She simply paid the bill and Cruz swung the heavy plastic bags over one arm, keeping one hand free. He had his gun tucked into the small of his back and he wanted to be able to get to it quickly.

He thought they would head back to the hotel but Meg turned the opposite direction. "I need a few more things," she said.

Half a block later, she pushed open the door of a lingerie store. High counters with partitions every couple of feet captured a sea of silk and lace. Bras. Panties. Holy crap, garter belts.

The dry cleaning bag brushed against a rack of nightgowns that rippled in response. He overcorrected and his other elbow knocked against a mannequin, wearing a little bit of nothing that would make a grown man beg. He grabbed a breast and managed to get it righted before it fell over.

He felt like a bull in a china shop but it was all worth it when Meg, for the first time since he'd knocked on her office door, smiled at him. "Asking for her number?" she mocked.

"Funny," he said. Meg had always loved pretty underwear. And he'd loved seeing her in it.

Buying it for her. The private modeling sessions that followed.

He could hear the air-conditioning going full blast but his neck felt hot. The store was full of women. There were only two men and they were dutifully following their wives or girlfriends around the room. Directly across the wide room was a door that probably led to a backroom and then to the alley. If he stood by the cash register, he'd have a good view of the room and both possible exits. "I'll wait up front," he said.

Meg took a shopping basket off the stack. "I won't be long."

He hoped not. His eyes were starting to water. Somebody was wearing enough perfume to knock an elephant on its butt.

Meg smelled the same. He wasn't sure exactly when he'd noticed that but it had been nagging at him. Her skin had always been so soft, so incredibly sexy, and her scent, some perfect combination of vanilla and her, had turned him on. Always.

Six months ago, he'd awakened after surgery, thinking, *Damn my leg hurts but at least I'm not dead,* and he'd known she was there. He'd lain in the bed, keeping his eyes closed, content just to let her scent surround him.

She was back. It had made getting shot worth it. A hundred times over.

She'd held his hand. He hadn't been in any shape to converse but that hadn't kept the thoughts from tumbling around in his drugged-up head. *I promise I'll be a better husband. I promise I'll be more in touch with what you need. I promise I'll be enough.*

But he hadn't had the opportunity to even try to deliver on those unspoken oaths. She'd held his hand, kissed his cheek, whispered goodbye and that was the last time he'd seen her until today.

Who'd have thought that he'd be standing around watching her buy underwear? No matter that every item Meg dropped into her basket caused the heat on his neck to branch out until his whole body felt warm. No matter that he felt like a damn teenager because he was getting hard. No matter what. His job was to watch her. He'd somehow failed her before. And that couldn't be changed. But he would not fail her with this.

He shifted the dry cleaning, folding it over one arm, letting it hang in front of him. When Meg came up to the counter to pay for her items, he kept his eyes moving around the room, away from where the cashier was diligently wrapping every item in tissue paper. There was only so much temptation he could take.

"Ready?" she asked.

Oh, yeah. Ready, aimed poorly and about to

fire. He opened the door, scanned the street and stepped out first. Meg followed and they walked back toward the hotel in silence. When they got to their rooms, he unlocked Meg's door and checked it before letting her enter. "Do you want to rest before we eat?" he asked.

She shook her head. "I'll take a fast shower. Will that work for you?"

What would really work for him was if she put on some of her new purchases and straddled his body and he—

"Cruz?"

"Yeah. Works for me."

MEG STOOD UNDER the shower and let the hot water attempt to work the tension out of her shoulders, her back. Her mind. It had only been seven hours since Cruz had stood in her doorway and already she was a bundle of conflicting emotions. She wanted him gone. She wanted him in her bed. She wanted him to understand that she wasn't his responsibility any longer. She wanted him to tease her and make her laugh like he used to.

Ping, pong. Up, down. Right, left. She was waffling more than a presidential candidate.

It had been so much easier to pretend that she didn't love him still when he'd been a thousand miles away. She could pretend that she'd moved on. She could pretend that she hadn't left everything that ever mattered back in Illinois.

The pretending she'd been doing—well that was merely drama class. Now that he was here, staying next door, committed to being her shadow, her performance needed to be worthy of a damn academy award.

She got out of the shower and towel-dried her short hair. When she'd been married, she'd worn it past her shoulders, taking the time to straighten the thick, naturally curly locks. That's how Cruz had liked it. She'd cut it the day after she'd come back from her vigil at his hospital bed that had begun with a call from Sam.

Cruz was shot. He's at the hospital. Not sure of his condition.

She'd taken the first plane from San Antonio to Chicago. They'd already been apart for six months but she'd known that she needed to be there.

Hadn't been able to do anything but stand over him, surrounded by humming machines and blinking lights, and will him to live. When she'd been sure he would, she'd left again, knowing for sure what she'd believed six months earlier when she'd left the first time. He was better off without her.

Perhaps cutting her hair had been symbolic of cutting the last thread that connected her to this man. Damn him for saying he liked it. He should have hated it.

Hated her.

Maybe he did. Maybe he wanted to walk away but he couldn't. He had always been guided by a sense of duty. That was what made him such a good cop. He'd been promoted through the ranks and had made detective faster than most but hardly anyone seemed to begrudge him the success. They knew he worked hard, pushed hard, made it tough for the bad guys.

She opened her dry cleaning and pulled out a simple black dress. She left the matching jacket on the hanger. Even at night, the temperature would hover near eighty. If they ate outside, she would roast in the jacket. She left her legs bare and slipped on the heels that she'd already worn for twelve hours.

Two sharps raps on the connecting door signified Cruz's arrival. She opened it and saw that he'd showered, too—the ends of his hair were still a little damp. He'd changed into a pair of gray cargo shorts and a white T-shirt.

"You look tired," he said.

Great. What every woman wanted to hear. "I'm fine." She crossed his room and opened the door. "You should definitely spend some time on the River Walk. It's really fabulous."

"I'm not here as a tourist, Meg."

"I know that," she said. He was here because she was an obligation. She was a tired-looking obligation. *Be still my heart.* "Look, let's just go."

While the evening air was still warm, the sun was low in the sky and had lost its intensity. The skyline was a wild combination of pinks and reds with a little purple creeping in. As they strolled past the open-air restaurants, sweet flower smells combined with the scent of rich food. The gentle murmur of conversation and laughter was punctuated by the rumble of the small guided riverboats filled with gawking tourists. The guide would fill their ears with facts and trivia about the city and the river and how the town had practically died out in the fifties before a few visionaries had figured out how to channel, literally, the area's greatest natural resource.

Texas wasn't for sissies. When she'd arrived a year earlier, they'd been in the middle of a horrific drought with wildfires burning across the state. Tourism dollars were tight and there was talk at the hotel that layoffs were imminent. Accepting that Mother Nature could be wicked, she and Scott had vowed to worry about the things they could control.

No guest left less than delighted. When there was the occasional complaint, either Meg or Scott or one of their highly trained managers immediately investigated and employed every service recovery trick in the book. As a result, there were almost all glowing reviews on the external websites and business had been better every month. With both of them working twelve hours a day, six days a week, they had managed to swim upstream and last quarter, their sales had been up thirty percent, year over year.

As a result, she hadn't spent much time strolling along the stone-lined riverbank and she wasn't much of a guide.

"What are you hungry for?" she asked. "There's Italian, Mexican, steaks and seafood. You name it, we've got it."

"Steak," he said.

Some things never changed.

And some things could not be changed. That's what had led them to this crazy place where they were almost as polite as strangers to one another but had a familiarity that no amount of time or distance could seem to diminish.

The restaurant she picked had indoor and outdoor seating. The hostess said both were available. Cruz raised an eyebrow, letting her make the choice. She always preferred to eat outside, no matter how hot. The young woman led them to an open spot and Cruz pulled out her chair. She glanced around and hoped that he didn't get the wrong idea. There were candles on all the tables and soft lights were strung through the branches of the trees that lined the sidewalk. It was romantic. The breeze blowing through the trees, skimming across her warm skin was almost sensual.

When the waiter came for drink orders, she chose red wine and Cruz got a beer. He ordered twelve ounces of Texas rib eye with a loaded baked potato and a Caesar salad. She ordered salmon and a side of broccoli.

"Some things never change," he said, as if he'd read her mind.

"I have a full day tomorrow," she said. "I'll start around seven and won't be done until late tomorrow night. I have an event."

He sipped his beer. "At work?"

"No. There's a not-for-profit in town called A Hand Up. Their mission is to help the recently incarcerated acclimate back into society by finding employers to offer six-month internships. The employers get a break financially because half the salary is paid by donations. The clients get a chance to demonstrate that they are walking the straight and narrow and can be good employees."

"And your connection with this group?"

"The hotel has offered several internships. I've been their contact."

He pushed his beer aside. "You're employing convicts?" he asked, his voice hard. "You don't think you might have mentioned that before now?"

She frowned at him. "Formerly incarcerated. They are vetted very thoroughly. We've had four clients, two have finished their rotation and two are more than halfway through. They've all been wonderful."

"I want their names."

"No. There's absolutely no reason to think that they have any grudge against me. It's known in advance that the assignments are six months long so they aren't surprised when the work ends. And they will be scared to death if some badass Chicago cop comes knocking on their door."

He picked up his beer and took a drink. "You think I'm a badass?"

She rolled her eyes. "Oh, for heaven's sake. Yes. As bad as they come."

"Where is the event?"

"Six blocks from here. At another hotel."

"You have to go?"

"I'm the main speaker."

The server delivered his salad. He worked his way through it. When he spoke again, he surprised her. "You'll do great."

"I'm nervous," she admitted. "I told the director

no initially but she was very insistent. Also, Scott thought it would be good publicity for our hotel."

He put down his fork without finishing his salad. "Good old Scott."

She ignored him and was grateful when the server delivered the main course. Cruz dug into his steak. She did little more than push her salmon around her plate. When the waiter came to clear their dishes and offer dessert, Cruz looked at her expectantly. Was he remembering that she'd always been a sucker for crème brûlée?

That was before. When it was fun to linger over dessert, to say deliberately provocative things over coffee, to see Cruz's eyes heat up, knowing that each whisper, each casual touch, would be collected upon in full.

Now she simply asked for the check. When the waiter slid it on the table, Cruz grabbed it. "I'll take that," he said.

Meg waited until the waiter had wandered off. "We should split it at least."

"No." Cruz pulled enough bills out of his pocket to cover the check and leave a generous tip. "Let's go."

It was close to ten and both sides of the River Walk were jammed with people. Young, old, fat, skinny, black, white—it was a crowd as diverse as the food choices. The restaurants and bars were still going strong, with their doors wide open. Music came from every direction. Rock. Blues. Jazz. Dueling pianos. Something for everybody.

Late spring was a beautiful time to be on the River Walk. While it was already hot, there had been more rain than last year. Annuals, in borders and beds, blossomed, gathering butterflies. Perennials, with their strong root system, crawled up the sides of brick walls, making the space intimate.

It was lovely. The huge trees, some growing right out of buildings, arched over the river, their branches swaying and dipping in the gentle nighttime breeze. Lights and candles and even the occasional flare from a cigarette gave the space warmth. The gentle murmur of conversation and the burst of a child's laughter or cry made it hum with energy.

It was probably too crowded for Cruz. She remembered the year that she'd managed to drag him Christmas shopping on the day after Thanksgiving. They'd been shopping on Michigan Avenue with a million other people determined to support the economy. He'd been as edgy as a wild animal. She'd teased him about having an aversion to spending money but in truth, she'd known that he was always on guard, always ready. And crowds limited his options—for escape, for attack. There was too much opportunity for collateral damage, he'd told her once.

They were almost back to the hotel when less than ten feet ahead of them, a group of six young men stumbled out of one of the Irish bars. Cruz caught her arm and pulled her behind him.

They were college-age and laughing and talking, using words that their mothers would not have approved of. Two started pretend boxing, circling each other, throwing weak punches. The others thought it was hilarious and performed some male ritual of back-slapping and hip-bumping.

Intent upon watching them, she missed the dark figure running up behind her and didn't have a chance to brace before she was shoved so hard from behind that she went airborne, right toward the river.

Chapter Four

Cruz whirled, lunged and managed to wrap a hand around one of Meg's flailing arms. He yanked her back, hauling her against his chest. Her face was white and her eyes big with fear.

She'd been inches from going into the dark green water. What the hell?

She pointed and he saw a black-clad figure running up the stairs that led to the street level. "Stay here," he said to her. He took the stairs two at a time, losing precious time as he dodged two women who were hauling a baby stroller down the steps.

He got up to the street level, scanned it in both directions and didn't see anything. Damn it. There were a hundred ways for someone to get away. Stores to step into. Cars to hide behind. Buses to board. The list was endless.

He pulled out his cell phone, dialed Myers and felt his blood pressure increase when the phone rang three times. On the fourth ring, the man answered, sounding a little out of breath.

"Myers."

"It's Cruz Montoya."

"Now what?" the man asked.

"Meg got pushed while we were walking along the River Walk. Subject ran up the stairs, disappeared into the 400 block of St. Mary's Street. Caucasian. About five-ten and one-sixty. Dressed all in black. Had a hat on so I couldn't see his hair. Moved fast so he's either young or in good shape."

"Got it. I'll call it in. Is Meg okay?"

"Yeah. This time. You need to find this bastard."

"We will." Myers hung up. Cruz took one more look up and down the street. Nothing jumped out at him. Then he looked over the cement railing to make sure Meg was all right. The young men were surrounding her, way too close for Cruz's liking. He charged back down the stairs.

He shouldered his way through the group and wrapped an arm around Meg's shoulders. "Okay?" he asked.

She nodded. "He got away?"

"Yeah." He turned to look at the group. "I've got this, guys," he said. He kept the tone light because he really didn't want to have to kick their drunk asses but he would if they didn't back off and stop looking at Meg like she was dessert.

Liquor-provided bravado caused one to step forward. "Hey, we were just having a conversation with the lady," he said, his words slurring.

Cruz shook his head. "She's done talking for the night. Excuse us."

He took a step forward and the guys were smart enough to let them through. He kept one arm around Meg's shoulders, holding her close.

She wouldn't have drowned. The water wasn't that deep. He'd learned that much from the brochure he'd scanned in the hotel lobby while he was waiting for Meg earlier. Probably only three or four feet. But then again, if she'd have hit her head on the stone walkway, it could have been a very different story. Anger burned in the pit of his stomach. She had been deliberately pushed. The guy was getting more aggressive each time. Crimes against property were one thing. A personal attack took it to a whole other level.

"I called Myers," he said. "I gave him a description, so maybe we'll get lucky."

"Did you get a good look at him?" she asked, sounding surprised.

"I saw enough to know that he's white, a little shorter and a little lighter than me, and he moves like a young guy."

"Good arm strength," she added, with a smile that trembled.

He tightened his grip and realized that it felt like the most natural thing in the world to have his arm around Meg. She fit. Always had. Always would.

Always wasn't the same as forever.

She made that more than clear when they got to the hotel and she moved away. Cruz let his arm drop and tried to ignore the sharp pain of disappointment. She probably didn't want Slater hearing that she'd been friendly with her ex.

"Will the list be ready yet?" Cruz asked.

"I'm sure it is."

She led him to her office. It was just as big and impressive as it had been earlier that day but this time, probably because he wasn't light-headed from just seeing her for the first time in a year, he noticed something else. It was bare, almost stark. Sure, there was the desk, credenza and matching chairs. But where was her collection of miniature glass giraffes? Or the Monet print that she loved? Or the brass bookends that she'd picked up cheap at a flea market but were so damn heavy that she'd had to give the guy an extra twenty bucks to carry them to her car?

"Where are your things?" he asked.

There was a slight hesitation before she answered. "Probably in a box somewhere that I never got around to unpacking," she said finally.

Maybe. But she wasn't making eye contact.

There was a manila folder on her chair. She opened it, scanned the contents and handed it to him. It was a list. Behind the single sheet, there was a stack of pictures. Head shots. Smiles. Happy new employees. He counted the pictures. "Only eight?" he asked.

"We have very low turnover," she said. "Others quit but these were the ones discharged."

He scanned the photos, separating white males from the rest of the bunch. There were three. Under each photo was a name and what he assumed was some kind of employee number.

He cross-referenced the pictures to the list and started sorting.

"What are you doing?" she asked.

"Thinking about motive," he said. "I'm putting them in order of tenure, most to least. With seniority comes paid time off and company contributions to retirement plans. Things a person might not be able to replace right away, even if he did find other work. A guy with ten years of experience is probably more pissed off when he loses his job than the guy with eight months of time into the job."

"Makes sense."

There was one who had eight years of experience, one that had three years, and one that had five months. He pointed to the man with eight years of experience. He looked to be in his early forties, with a thin face, dark hair and thick black glasses. "What's this guy's story?" he asked.

"Mason Hawkins. Pretty quiet at work, although it was known by most everybody that he wasn't all that happy with his job responsibilities. He applied for a couple higher-level positions but was never the chosen candidate. His attitude got in his way."

"What was his job?"

"He was an accounts payable specialist and he made sure our bills were paid. Now, most invoices get paid electronically. Bank transfers from our account to our vendor's account. He was fired because he processed invoices to vendors that didn't exist. He'd deposited over thirty thousand into his own checking account over a period of eight months before he had the bad luck to need an emergency appendectomy which required his boss to step in for a few days. Bye-bye appendix. Bye-bye job."

"Did you get the money back?"

"He was about five thousand short. He's making monthly payments in lieu of us pressing charges."

Cruz made a note of the man's address. "What about Tom Looney?"

Meg studied the picture of the man, maybe early

thirties, who had his straight brown hair pulled back in a stubby ponytail. "He worked in maintenance. Had a great record until he suddenly started missing work. Ultimately he missed so much time we had no choice but to let him go. I heard a rumor after he left that he'd lost his house."

"Everybody's got a story," Cruz said, shaking his head.

"It's what makes management really hard," she said. "For every story you know, there are six that you don't. It makes making exceptions really difficult."

"Good judgment. Isn't that what managers are supposed to have?"

"Easy to say. Suppose the manager knows that somebody is late for work because they're working a second job to pay for their kid's medical bills. He might want to cut that employee some slack. But the minute he does, that's when he finds out that three other people are working second jobs— each with their own set of sad circumstances. So the manager fires the guy for being late and feels horrible about it or he lets it go and upper management is breathing down his neck for setting a poor precedent."

"You're pretty high up in the management structure. Don't breathe so heavy."

She smiled. "I'm working on that," she said.

She was being too hard on herself. She was one of the good guys. Always had been. Hell, one Thanksgiving, there had been people sitting at his table that didn't even speak English. She'd discovered in casual conversation that some of the housekeeping staff had no plans for the day and that had been the end of his opportunity to watch a football game in his shorts with a beer in one hand and a pretzel bowl close to the other.

That's what made it so hard to believe that somebody at work would want to harm her. But it was the most logical explanation.

He picked up the last of the three photos. "What about this one?"

Meg looked at the picture of a man with dark hair cut in a buzz and a short-clipped full beard. He had very blue eyes, silver-rimmed glasses and looked to be mid-twenties. "Troy Blakely worked for a short time in security. He was let go after he got in a prolonged shouting match with one of our guests."

"What happened?"

"We were never quite sure how it started. Troy was using the exercise room. We allow all of our employees to do so on their off hours, although they are clearly instructed to defer to our guests and that they should give up machines if guests are waiting."

"Pretty reasonable."

"We think so. Anyway, a female guest was working out in our exercise room and decided to switch machines. Troy was in the room and must have wanted the same machine. He supposedly started yelling at her."

"Supposedly?"

"Yes. When our human resources manager investigated the complaint, she was unable to confirm exactly what happened in the exercise room. There were no witnesses."

"So there were lots of machines probably available?"

"Yes. That's what made this so weird. The guest said that she got scared and decided to leave the room. Well, the altercation between the two of them continued out into the hallway. We know this for sure because we caught it on camera. What we saw matched the guest's story. She was trying to end the confrontation by literally running down the hallway. But Troy kept following her, kept yelling at her. He was waving his arms and pointing his finger at her. Very aggressive behavior. Fortunately, he never actually touched the woman so there was no assault or battery but it was clear that he had some kind of anger management problem. No hotel can afford to keep an employee who demonstrates those types of behaviors. He was terminated immediately."

Cruz sighed. When he'd first become a cop, he'd been surprised at how damn angry people were. Angry about their lot in life and they took it out on coworkers, spouses and their children. Sometimes they were sorry afterward. The really sick ones thought they were justified.

He stuffed the photos and the list back in the manila folder. "Let's get some shut-eye," he said.

It took them five minutes to get to their rooms. She was silent for the whole trip. When she unlocked her door, he followed her in. "Get your things," he said.

"What?"

"You're sleeping in that room," he said, pointing toward his room.

She bristled, drawing up to her full five feet six inches. "I am *not* sleeping with you," she said.

He counted to ten before replying. It didn't help. "Yeah, I don't remember asking but I do remember you telling me a year ago that you weren't interested." It was petty and probably juvenile but damn, he was tired. He'd been up for almost twenty-four hours.

She seemed to shrink, like a balloon suddenly losing air. "But…" she began.

"Until we know who is behind this, everybody

is a suspect, including the person who gave you the keys to this room. If somebody gets the bright idea of breaking in, a second or two of confusion will be all I need."

"I got the key from a woman that I've known for over a year. She's not going to harm me."

"Everybody is a suspect. Including your boss."

"Don't be ridiculous," she scoffed.

It was the second time she'd accused him of being ridiculous. The first had been after he'd said she wasn't in charge of who got to vacation in Texas. Hell, she hadn't even begun to see ridiculous. He had enough in him to go all night. Had been saving it up for the past year.

But given that he didn't want to listen to her defend Boy Scout Scott, he tempered the urge. "Can we just go to bed? You, in there and me, in here. Separate but equal. Very politically incorrect."

She massaged her temples and it reminded him of the day she'd had. She had dark shadows under her pretty eyes.

He shut up.

She let out a breath that she had evidently been holding. "All right," she said.

He almost sighed in response. He was dead on his feet and he didn't want to fight with her. Had always hated to see her upset and had been miserable the few times in their marriage when they'd argued about something stupid. She grabbed her dry cleaning out of the closet and the sack that had her other things. "My clothes go with me," she said. Then she left, partially closing the door between the two rooms.

It opened again after just seconds and she tossed his bag into the room. It toppled end over end, before stopping when it hit the wall. It made him smile. Now who was being ridiculous?

He brushed his teeth and splashed some water on his face. Then he took his shirt off. He left his cargo shorts on because a good cop never got caught with his pants down or off. He pulled back the bedspread, turned off his light and lay back on the big bed.

It took her four minutes and eighteen seconds to turn her light off. Once she did, he could hear her sheets rustle. What the hell was she wearing to bed? She hadn't bought pajamas. So, maybe it was one of her fancy new bra and panty sets.

Or maybe she was naked.

He closed his eyes and rested his forearm across the bridge of his nose, as if that would somehow be an extra level of protection against the images that were playing in his head.

MEG WOKE UP when she heard a knock on the door. She jerked up in bed and saw Cruz standing in the doorway between the two rooms, a coffee cup in hand. He was dressed in a fresh shirt and cargo shorts and his hair was still damp.

"What time is it?" she asked.

"Seven," he said, his voice husky. "You slept in your dress?"

Cruz Montoya was one of the sexiest men to walk the planet and he turned her on. Always. Still. And there was no way in hell she was letting him know that and double no-way that she was going to act upon it.

So she'd gone to bed with the only armor she had. "I thought the room might be chilly."

"You can always turn down the air-conditioning," he said.

"Whatever. I better get dressed."

"Coffee?" he said. "I just made a second pot."

Cruz loved coffee. And drank way more than he should. On the weekends it hadn't been unusual that he'd get through two pots before she ever poked her head out of the bedroom. "No, thanks," she said.

"What?"

She'd given up coffee when she'd moved to Texas. The smell of it had kept too many memories fresh. "It bothers my stomach," she said.

"Have you seen a doctor?" he asked, sounding concerned.

"So that he could tell me *good job?* Drinking coffee is a vice, not a virtue."

Cruz rolled his eyes. "Once you get showered and dressed, I'll walk you to your office. By the way, I called your boss early this morning."

"Why?"

"'Cause we're buddies."

She rolled her eyes this time.

"Because I wanted him to know what happened on the River Walk. I suggested that he assign a security guard outside your office. He said to consider it done."

"Do you really think that's necessary?"

"I wouldn't have asked if I didn't."

She wanted to argue that it was a waste of a resource but knew it was probably useless. Cruz had convinced Scott and there was no way she could persuade both of them. "Then what are your plans?"

"I'm going to track down Mason Hawkins, Tom Looney and Troy Blakely."

She'd known Hawkins and Looney pretty well. They'd been at their jobs when she'd gotten hired. She knew Blakely less well. He'd come a couple months after her and his tenure had been short. She'd had no bad interactions with any of the men, hadn't even been there when they'd been fired. Yes, she was administration but surely that wasn't enough for one of them to hate her.

But somebody did. If it wasn't hate, it was something close. The only person who really had a reason to hate her was Cruz and she knew he was innocent.

Well, Cruz wasn't the only person. It was crazy to think that this had something to do with what had happened in Maiter but she couldn't afford to be stupid about it. She was definitely going to need to talk with Detective Myers about what had happened twenty years ago.

"What are you going to say to Hawkins, Looney and Blakely if you find them?"

"When, not if," he said. "I'll find them. And I'll have a reasonable conversation with them unless I think they're involved in this. Then I'm going to start cracking heads."

"Cruz," she warned. "Detective Myers made it clear. He's the investigator on this case. Not you."

"Then he better stick close to my heels," Cruz said. He backed away from the doorway. "Knock when you're ready." He pulled the door halfway shut and Meg heard the television click on.

She got out of bed, pulled the tags off her new underwear and grabbed a freshly dry-cleaned suit. She carried everything into the bathroom with her.

Thirty minutes later, she knocked on the adjoining door. Cruz didn't look startled at the interruption and she had the sense that no matter how quiet she'd been in her room, that he'd heard and tracked every movement.

He saw too much. It made it even more important that she hide her thoughts from him.

"That's a nice color on you," he said, looking at her peach suit.

"Thank you," she said. She couldn't remember Cruz ever saying anything about her clothes. He'd always just let his eyes do the talking. Heat. Awareness. Want.

This felt awkward. Maybe because it seemed awkward for Cruz. Like he was saying it because he should and Cruz never did or said anything just because he was supposed to.

They left the room and walked toward the elevator. "You going to eat breakfast?" he asked.

"We keep some fruit and bagels in the executive break area. I'll just grab something later. If you're hungry, several places along the River Walk serve breakfast. Plus there are more choices up on the street level."

"I'll figure something out," he said.

When they got to her office door, she saw Tim Burtiss sitting on a chair outside the door. He stood up when he saw them. "Good morning, Meg," the man said.

"Hi, Tim." She turned to Cruz. "This is Security Officer Tim Burtiss. Tim was our associate of the month in January. Tim, this is my ex-husband, Cruz Montoya."

Cruz shook the young man's hand. Tim was practically beaming and Meg was happy that she'd been able to slip in something about his recent recognition. Not only did it make the young man feel good but hopefully it would also send a subtle message to Cruz that this was one of the hotel's best security guards. He didn't need to worry.

It must have worked because Cruz didn't ask him about his experience, to drop and give him twenty or to demonstrate that he knew how to use the baton that was clipped to his belt. All he said was, "I need to touch base with Meg's secretary and then we can talk."

Great. He wanted to meet Charlotte. Which would prompt the woman to ask about a hundred questions and she'd have answers for none of them.

Meg opened the door. Charlotte sat at her desk, a cup of coffee in one hand, a telephone in the other. She looked at Meg, then at Cruz, and told the person that she'd have to return the call. She put down the telephone with a soft thud.

"Good morning, Charlotte," Meg said. She took a deep breath. "I wanted to introduce you to Cruz. Cruz Montoya. My ex-husband. Cruz, this is Charlotte Anderson."

To Charlotte's credit, she showed almost no

reaction to learning that her boss had been married but had never mentioned it. Perhaps her lip quivered just a little and her eyes widened but other than that, she was the perfect example of professional control, as always. "Mr. Montoya," she said. "It's a pleasure to meet you."

"Cruz is a police officer in Chicago and has been in contact with Detective Myers regarding the incidents." Meg shifted her attention to Cruz. "Charlotte is aware of the telephone call, the note and the damage to my car and apartment." She deliberately didn't mention the River Walk shove and was grateful when Cruz didn't, either.

"Charlotte pulled together the list of names that you reviewed," Meg added.

"Thanks," Cruz said. "Security Officer Tim Burtiss is going to be sitting outside the door. He's going to need to know who is expected. Can you work with him on that?"

"Of course. Anything to keep Meg safe."

"Great. Here's my cell number in case you need to reach me." He reached for a yellow sticky pad on Charlotte's desk and scribbled down the number. He turned to leave and Meg followed him. Tim Burtiss stood up again.

Cruz nodded at him. "Charlotte will touch base with you on who is expected today. Nobody else gets past you."

"Yes, sir."

"Don't let her leave. If she tries to, tackle her," Cruz added.

The young officer looked at Meg and the tips of his ears got pink.

"He's kidding," she said.

"Only a little," Cruz responded. He turned toward her. "Be smart, Meg. Please."

She was going to be in her office with a guard. Cruz was the one who was going to be out, asking questions, maybe making people uncomfortable. He was the one who needed to be careful. She put her arm out, touched his shoulder.

He jerked back.

Had he felt the heat? The spark of connection? "Right back at ya," she said, knowing it was lame. But the need to touch, the need to hold him tight, was almost overbearing.

He nodded. "I'll see you tonight."

She watched him walk away.

"Promise?" she whispered so quietly that even Officer Burtiss couldn't have heard her.

Chapter Five

Cruz ate an egg-and-potato burrito and used his smart phone to research A Hand Up. Meg might be convinced that the jailbirds had no reason to harm her but Cruz had been putting scum away for enough years that he didn't have as much faith.

He found a contact number, made the call, and worked his way up the chain of command until he was talking to the head honcho, Beatrice Classen. He introduced himself as Meg's husband.

"I didn't realize that Meg was married," she said.

He thought about correcting her but decided it might work against him. "I need to talk with you about some problems that Meg has been having."

He went on to explain about her car and apartment and the recent incident at the River Walk. When he suggested that he was concerned about former prisoners working at the hotel, Beatrice did two things in quick succession. She expressed her concern over Meg's safety and vehemently denied that her clients had anything to do with it.

He hadn't expected her to do anything else. She'd probably worked hard to get businesses to sign on to employing those recently released from jail. A business might be willing to write a check to support the program but to actually get them to agree to offering up a job, that was probably a tougher sell. Beatrice no doubt didn't want some husband coming along and spoiling things.

"Mr. Montoya, I'd be happy to assist in any way that I could," she said.

"I'd like to review their files," Cruz said. "And see a photo ID."

"It's sort of a bad day. We're getting ready for our banquet. I need to be at the LaMadra Hotel most of the day. I was just getting ready to leave my office."

He wasn't waiting. "I'll meet you at LaMadra in a half hour," he said.

The woman paused. "I suppose I can bring the files with me," she said finally, clearly resigned to the fact that this was one more thing she was going to have to squeeze into her day.

Cruz finished his breakfast, had another cup of coffee, and headed for the hotel.

The place was even bigger than the BJM, with more glass and shiny steel. He asked a woman at the front desk where the A Hand Up banquet was being held that night and she pointed him toward the elevators. "Fourth floor," she said.

He walked into the ballroom. Employees were setting up tables, arranging chairs, testing a sound system. Everybody ignored him, which really pissed him off. Not only because it was wasting his time but more important, it meant that any weirdo could come in and nobody would notice.

Cruz watched to see who might be in charge. There was a guy with a clipboard who seemed pretty intent upon barking out orders. Cruz tapped him on the shoulder. "Beatrice Classen?" he asked.

The guy pointed to the head table, where a woman wearing a bright pink sweat suit was jawing on some poor guy about the fact that the head table needed a skirt. As he got closer, it became apparent that the problem was that it needed to be ivory, not white.

"Ms. Classen?" he inquired.

"Yes."

"Cruz Montoya," he said.

Her hair was thin and had lots of static electricity, making pieces stick out as if she'd poked her finger in a light socket. She probably weighed in at about two-fifty, making her almost as round as she was tall. "I have your information right here," she said, pointing at a manila folder on the table.

He leafed through the photos. One Hispanic, one black and two white men. He studied the white men. They were full poses, not just head shots. "This guy looks pretty tall. You know his height?" he asked, holding up one.

"Well, everyone is tall compared to me, Mr. Montoya. However, I did hear him mention once that he was six-six."

Cruz set it aside and picked up the other photo. "Tell me about this guy."

"Oscar Warren. He was part of the first rotation so he hasn't been at the hotel for several months."

"What was he in prison for?"

"Aggravated arson. He set his girlfriend's apartment on fire after he found her in bed with another woman."

Another woman. It had been a punch when Meg had left him to follow another man across the country. Would it be better or worse if the woman you loved suddenly switched teams? Maybe he was pissed off at all women now, hated the whole breed. "Have you seen him since he ended his assignment at Meg's hotel?"

"Of course. We arranged for his second rotation. He's at a food pantry, on Fourth and Taylor."

"I appreciate you showing me these," Cruz said.

"I was sorry to hear about Meg's trouble. But I know that none of these men were involved.

Clients of our program are vetted very carefully and none of them want to do something foolish and end up back in prison."

He looked around the room. "Looks as if it's going to be a nice event. Did people have to buy tickets in advance?"

"Yes. We sold tickets at multiple locations around town as well as online. I was thrilled when we sold out days ago."

Tickets in advance. That was good. It meant that bad guys, on a whim, a dare, or a meth high couldn't decide to walk in and start causing trouble. But given that there were multiple access points, Meg's tormentor simply would have needed to plan ahead a bit to have a good seat, one with a clear view of the stage.

"When will Meg give her speech?"

"We'll have dinner first, then the awards presentation to both participants in the program and to business leaders who have helped keep the program alive. Then Meg's speech will close out the event." She studied him. "I was sure that I'd told Meg she could bring a guest."

"You did," he said. "But I thought I was going to have to work. I just found out this morning that I'm free."

Beatrice's eyes sparkled. "You know, Mr. Montoya, we still have one available seat at the head table. It would be a wonderful surprise for Meg."

He wasn't so sure about that but after last night, there was no way he intended to let Meg go to an evening event without protection. Slater could no doubt be convinced to keep a security officer with her. Jerk might even volunteer for duty himself.

Not a chance that Cruz was going to let that happen.

"That would be great," he said. "I appreciate it."

CRUZ DROVE TO the food pantry. He found Oscar unpacking cans of peaches. The man was the right height and weight and he was throwing around the heavy cases of canned fruit with ease.

Good arm strength, Meg had said.

"Mr. Warren," Cruz said. "I'm Detective Cruz Montoya and I'm investigating a series of incidents that have occurred at or near the BJM Hotel." He didn't want to show too much of his hand too soon.

The man shifted his weight from foot to foot. He seemed nervous. Given that he'd recently done time, Cruz realized that just having a cop want to chat might be enough to raise the blood pressure.

"I haven't worked at the hotel for months," he said.

"I know that. Where were you last night around nine?"

"Home."

"Anybody there with you?"

The man shook his head. "I live alone," he said.

"What about yesterday morning?"

"I was here, working."

"Anybody verify that?" Cruz asked.

The man pointed to a woman wearing blue jeans and a gray T-shirt. "Tracy runs the place. She was here, too."

He was working for a woman. Maybe he wasn't too bent out of shape.

It took Tracy less than five minutes to verify that Oscar had indeed been working the previous day. She showed Cruz a handwritten time sheet. "I got in early yesterday, about six. Oscar came in at his regular time."

Cruz glanced at the sheet and saw that Oscar started work shortly after eight. Cruz would have much preferred that the time records were from a time clock with an automatic time stamp, rather than handwritten. He could have trusted them more. Still, it was a small place. Tracy probably had a handle on when her employees arrived.

Meg had said that she'd left her condo around seven. That wouldn't have given him much time to trash the place. Plus somehow between her arrival at work and noon, he'd have had to get over to the hotel, bang up her car and plant the bad fish.

"He was here the whole day?" Cruz asked.

Tracy nodded. "All day. He did have to run out midmorning. We got an unexpected contribution from one of the big grocery stores in town. They had a bunch of canned goods that were coming up on their expiration date. The need in this community is pretty great so we wanted to get it picked up and sorted, then distributed as quickly as possible."

"Where is the grocery store?"

The woman walked over to a large map that was tacked to a cork bulletin board. "Here," she said.

Cruz looked at the map, figured out where the hotel was in relation to the grocery store and realized that the two were less than fifteen blocks apart. "How long was he gone?"

Now Tracy was looking at him oddly. "Less than an hour. Is something wrong, Detective?" she asked. "This is a small place, with very few employees. We don't want any trouble."

If the guy was telling the truth, Cruz was close to screwing up any hopes of him keeping this particular job. "No. Nothing's wrong," he said. "Thank you for your help."

Cruz nodded at Oscar as he left the building. The man didn't respond.

Cruz got in his car and started driving toward the grocery store. Once inside, Cruz gave a woman at the service counter his business card and she went off to look for the manager. Cruz waited impatiently.

The manager was a young black man dressed in a white shirt, dark pants and a tie. His head was totally shaved and it reminded Cruz that he should get a haircut. The man shook Cruz's hand. "Detective Montoya," he said. "What can I do for you?"

"I'm attempting to verify the time that a pickup was made at your store yesterday. A man came from the food pantry and got some canned goods."

"We can check. We log that kind of activity." The young man led him through the store, back to the dock area. There were big trucks and it smelled like diesel fuel. It was hot in comparison to the air-conditioned store.

The manager pulled a clipboard off a hook and ran his finger across a line. "He arrived at nine-thirty and left here at ten-ten."

With travel time, that would have given him very little time to get to Meg's car. Impossible? No. But not likely if Tracy's memory was correct.

"Thank you," he said. He returned to his car and immediately opened the file for the employees who had been terminated by the hotel within the past year. He plugged the first address into his GPS.

He found Mason Hawkins at home. The neighborhood was middle-class, with small ranch-style homes. None of them had garages and most had cars parked in the driveway or in front, along the street.

There were no vehicles in Hawkins's driveway. An old white van, with its front tires beached on the curb, sat in front, halfway between Hawkins's house and the neighbor's.

Cruz knocked on the wooden door and waited a full minute before it slowly swung open. Hawkins wore boxer shorts, black socks and a cardigan sweater that zipped up the front. His hair was dirty and he was holding an open bag of potato chips.

Cruz noted it all but he wasn't overly interested in the trappings. A man could change his wardrobe, alter his appearance and even take on a different persona. He couldn't change his physical size as easily. And Hawkins was close enough to five-ten, one-sixty, that Cruz stayed interested. He took stock of Hawkins's thigh muscles and saw that they didn't scream *slacker* in the same way his outfit did.

"Yes?" Hawkins said.

"I'm Cruz Montoya." The man showed no reaction to Cruz's name. That didn't sway Cruz one way or the other. If Hawkins was behind last night's push, he probably knew that Meg's ex-husband was in town and he'd had plenty of time to prepare for a visit from him or the cops.

"Whatever you're selling, I'm not buying," Hawkins said and tried to swing the door shut.

Cruz put his foot out, stopping the momentum. "You used to work at the BJM Hotel."

The man glared at him. "I can't imagine what business that is of yours," he said. Hawkins was trying for tough but it wasn't working. He'd flinched when Cruz had said the hotel's name.

Cruz leaned forward, getting in Hawkins's face. He wasn't conducting an investigation. He didn't need to hold his cards close. Myers would kick his ass if he found out about the visit. The detective's primary motivation would be to gather enough evidence to prosecute someone for the crimes that had been committed; Cruz's interest was more personal—he simply wanted it to stop before it got more violent and Meg got hurt.

"Oh, it's definitely my business," he said, his voice low. "I care about Meg Montoya. And if I was to find out that you had any intent of causing her even a minute of distress, I would be pissed off. Got that? Really pissed off. Then I become your worst nightmare."

Hawkins's hand, the one holding the potato chip bag, was shaking. The plastic crinkled. "I gave BJM eight years of my life. They paid me lousy and wasted my talent. I've got a master's degree in accounting and I was paying monthly invoices and processing payroll. A high school graduate could have done it. They owed me."

"Not my issue," Cruz said. "Meg Montoya is my concern."

"I've got nothing against her. Her boss, that's another story. He's a jerk. Said he was doing me a favor by not pressing charges. I'm about to lose my house and I can't find another job, not without a reference from the place I worked for eight years. I might be better off in jail."

"Guys like you don't do well in jail. You're dessert after a big meal." Cruz could tell that Hawkins got the drift by the look in the man's eyes. He figured it wasn't the first time he'd reflected upon what his life might be like in prison. That was undoubtedly why he was writing monthly checks to BJM.

Cruz leaned forward. "If I find out that you're lying to me, I'm going to come back here and strangle you with one of your black socks. Do we have an understanding?"

"I just want to get on with my life," Hawkins said. He moved to close the door and this time, Cruz let him.

He walked down the sidewalk back to his rental car. Hawkins was bitter and thoroughly convinced that he'd been screwed. That was enough to keep him on the short list of suspects. But even if he wouldn't admit it, he had to know that he was lucky that BJM hadn't pressed charges. Would he be stupid enough to do something else that could land him in jail?

Cruz didn't know. But he thought he'd gotten his point across. Now he needed to keep working his list of suspects.

He used the GPS in his car and realized that Troy Blakely's apartment was within fifteen minutes of Hawkins's house. When he got there, he quickly realized that finding this guy might not be quite so easy.

None of the inhabitants at the rat hole of a building in downtown San Antonio had ever heard of Troy Blakely. It took Cruz another two hours to track down the landlord who confirmed that he'd never rented to anyone by that name.

Which meant that he'd falsified his address on his employment paperwork. There was no good reason to do that.

Chapter Six

He called Meg. The phone was picked up on the second ring. "Meg Montoya's office. Charlotte speaking."

"This is Cruz Montoya. May I speak to Meg?"

"I'm sorry, Mr. Montoya. Meg is in a meeting. Can I help you with something?"

He debated asking Charlotte for the information but didn't want to tip his hand to anybody. Who knew if there was any connection between Charlotte and Blakely? Even though Blakely hadn't worked there long, security personnel did interact with administrative staff on a pretty routine basis. It was likely their paths had crossed. Plus there was something about Charlotte, something that hadn't seemed quite right this morning. She was nice enough but when he'd mentioned that Slater had assigned a security officer, there had been a strange look in her eyes. It was logical that she was freaked out about the possibility of danger in her work space but he wasn't sure that was it.

"Can you just ask Meg to call me when she gets the chance?" Cruz requested.

Cruz disconnected and used the GPS in his rental car to find his next stop. Ten minutes later, he pulled into a strip mall and located the store. He hadn't expected to go shopping in San Antonio but in less than twenty-four hours, this would be his second time.

It took him an hour to get what he needed. Ten minutes of that was spent picking out stuff, the other fifty minutes, along with a hundred-dollar bill, was enough for the owner to hem the pants on the spot.

After that, he went looking for Tom Looney. He drove to the address that the hotel had on file but didn't have high hopes. Meg had said that the word on the street was that Looney had lost his house.

It could not have been much to lose, he decided, once he made his last turn. The narrow street was three blocks off a service road and the houses were double-wides on cement blocks.

He found the mailbox, parked and got out of the car. A skinny black dog, lying near the front steps, looked up but didn't bother to *get* up, evidently deciding he wasn't worth the effort. He knocked on the door and waited several minutes in the blistering heat. Sweat ran down the back of his neck.

Finally, the door opened. An elderly woman,

probably mid-seventies, wearing a housedress and no shoes stared at him. "Hello," she said. Her body might have been frail but her voice was strong, confident.

"Afternoon, ma'am. I'm looking for Tom Looney."

"You must be a bill collector. I'll tell you what I told everybody else. I ain't seen Bertie's boy since the day I moved in."

"Bertie?"

"Tommy's momma. My second cousin. I bought this trailer from them when he started having money trouble. And before you go and ask, I don't know where Bertie and Tommy went. They didn't say and I didn't ask. Good day." She closed the door.

Cruz could have stuck his foot out, like he'd done with Mason Hawkins. But he knew it wouldn't do any good. First, he didn't want to bully an old woman and second, she was either telling the truth and she didn't know or she was lying and she knew but wouldn't tell. Either way, she wasn't going to be helpful.

His cell phone was ringing as he walked back to the car. He glanced at the number and recognized it. As quick as that, his stupid heart started to beat faster. Not so long ago, he'd gotten a couple of these calls every day. Just a quick check-in, a sweet *I was thinking of you.* "Hi, Meg," he said.

"I got your message from Charlotte," she said. Her tone was brisk, businesslike.

He could see her sitting at her fancy wood desk, her short hair pushed behind her ears, maybe a half-empty cup of coffee at her side. No. Scratch that. She'd given up coffee. Just one small sign of how much had changed.

"How's it going?" he asked.

"Fine. Busy day," she said. "How's it…uh… going for you?"

"Pretty good. I have run into a snag with Troy Blakely and Tom Looney, though. I need more information on them. Previous addresses. Past employers. Stuff that would either be on their employment applications or maybe even background check authorization forms."

She didn't respond.

"You still there, Meg?"

"I've already given you a lot of information. It doesn't seem right that I would dig deeper into confidential files to help myself."

Meg had always been a rule-follower. Had never wanted to use her position to her advantage. Once, when she'd gotten pulled over for a busted taillight, he'd been pissed off that she hadn't mentioned to the cop that her husband was also one of Chicago's finest. It was practically a guarantee that she'd have driven on, ticket-free. Everybody did stuff like that.

Not Meg.

"Look, I'm not trying to steal either one of their identities. Once I find them and know that they're not behind this, I'll have short-term memory problems and everything I know will be forgotten."

She sighed. "I'll have to get the file from the human resources department. Their offices are down the hall."

"I'll hold," he said.

Eight minutes later, he had information he hoped would help. He thought he had enough time to check out a couple of Blakely's previous employers before he needed to head back to the hotel. "In case I need more information, what time are you leaving the office?" he asked, hoping he wasn't being too obvious.

"By four. I need time to get dressed for the dinner. I'll have to take a cab to the event since my car is still out of commission."

She wouldn't be in the cab alone. But he didn't want to have that argument now. "Okay. I'll see you later," he said.

He programmed the address of Smitty's Gemstones into his GPS. Blakely had worked security for Smitty's before joining BJM. The store was in downtown San Antonio, nestled between other small retailers. When he opened the door, the lighting was dim, the carpet had seen better days and the man standing inside, arms folded across his chest, didn't look friendly.

Cruz ignored the guy and walked toward the older woman standing behind the counter. Here the lighting was a little better but dim enough that a customer might have difficulty picking up any flaws in the massive amount of jewelry and loose gemstones stuffed in the glass display cases.

"Can I help you?" she asked. Her tone was businesslike, indicating she liked buyers, not lookers. She was on the downside of fifty and had rings on every finger.

"I hope so," Cruz said, flashing her a smile. "I'm looking for somebody who used to work for you. Troy Blakely."

The woman frowned. "A friend of yours?"

Cruz went with his instinct and shook his head. "I've never met him. But I want to talk to him about some trouble a friend of mine is having."

"Is he behind this trouble?"

"I don't know," Cruz said. This woman looked like she could smell a line a mile away.

"Well, I wouldn't be surprised if he was. I think the guy has a screw loose. But I can't help you. I haven't seen him since he quit a year ago."

"What did he do to make you think he had a screw loose?"

The woman shook her head. "I caught him going through my files, writing down home addresses of people who'd left jewelry here to be appraised. When one of those houses got broken into, I figured he needed to go."

"Did you tell the police?"

The woman shook her head. "First of all, I didn't have any proof. Second of all, it would have been bad publicity for the store."

Cruz wasn't surprised and truth be told, not overly critical. He understood why people didn't want to become involved. Maybe the woman had been afraid of Blakely and worried that he'd turn on her if he suspected that she'd reported him to the police. Certainly odder things happened. Every day. "And you haven't seen him since then?"

"Nope."

It was another dead end. He was getting tired of them. "Thank you for your time," he said.

"No problem." The woman floated her hand in the air, gesturing toward the display cases. "Nobody at home you'd like to buy a small gift for?"

Over the years, he'd bought Meg an engagement ring and maybe a few pairs of earrings for Christmas or her birthday. He could certainly have done better. He glanced around, and walked over to a case where the lighting was better, the presentation nicer. A necklace caught his eye. It was a large blue stone, surrounded by small diamonds.

"That's my good stuff, honey. I hope she's worth it."

Twenty minutes later he was back at the hotel. It was ten minutes before four. He parked, practically jogged to Meg's office, and didn't really relax until he saw that the security guard was still sitting outside. "Hi, Tim," he said. "How'd it go today?"

The young man shrugged. "Fine."

"Nothing unusual?"

"No, sir."

"Okay, I'll take it from here," Cruz said.

"Sounds good to me. I always like getting out a little early on Friday nights."

Cruz opened the office door. Charlotte was standing at the copy machine, her back to the door. She glanced over her shoulder. "Mr. Montoya?" she said, her tone even more severe than when Meg had introduced them this morning. "I didn't realize that Meg expected you back."

"I got done a little early and thought I'd check in. Everything okay here?"

"Yes," she said, as if terribly insulted that he thought that she was lax enough to allow anything bad to happen on her watch. She waved her hand toward Meg's office. "She is just finishing up a meeting with Mr. Slater."

Cruz glared at the closed office door. Yeah, meeting. Right. "Mind if I have a seat?" he asked, nodding his head toward one of the leather chairs in the small waiting area.

"Of course not," she said. She finished making her copies and returned to her desk. She carefully labeled several file folders and stacked everything neatly on the corner of her desk. "I guess Meg is lucky to have her own private investigator," she said. "Very convenient."

"I don't think there's anything convenient about having both your car and your apartment trashed," he said.

"You're right. It's all shocking, really. The world is a bad place sometimes."

Her words were fine but there was something that wasn't. He just couldn't put his finger on it. And that worried him. His obsession with finding Meg's tormentor was screwing with his normally good judgment.

Meg's office door swung open. Slater had his back to Cruz, his arm braced against the office door, like he was posing for the cover of *GQ*. "Good luck tonight," Slater said.

"I'm nervous," Meg said. Her voice was faint, as if she was still behind her desk. "I've never talked to five hundred people before."

"Just look out and imagine the audience naked—they won't be nearly as intimidating. By the way," he said as he chuckled, "I think the BJM table is near the front."

Cruz wanted to cough up his lunch.

Meg laughed nervously. Cruz heard it but he was focused on Charlotte. She wasn't laughing. Her lips were clamped together and she gripped an empty file folder so tightly that her fingers were turning white.

Slater turned, walked out, and Meg followed. She had a garment bag folded over one arm. Slater nodded at him but didn't extend a greeting.

"I didn't realize you were here," Meg said. "I'm sure Charlotte took good care of you, though."

"My pleasure," Charlotte said. Her face was relaxed and she calmly laid the file folder on the corner of her desk with the others. She got up, walked over to the door and opened it. "Let's get you out of here, Meg. You'll need time to get ready."

"You, too," Meg protested. "You're at the BJM table, right? I'm going to need you cheering me on."

"I'll be there. But if you have just a minute, Scott, I've got some invoices that need your approval."

"Okay," Scott said. "See you later, Meg."

Cruz fell into step next to Meg. "What's in the bag?" he asked.

"My dress for tonight. Fortunately, it had needed some alterations and when I'd picked it up earlier this week from the tailor, I'd left it hanging in my office closet. Otherwise, I probably wouldn't have anything to wear tonight."

"I can carry it," he said.

"It's not that heavy," she said and continued walking. She hadn't gone more than four steps when Cruz spoke again.

"Five hundred people. This is a bad idea, you know. Somebody wants to harm you and you're going to be on a stage."

"Behind a podium. Nobody is going to try anything there. Too many witnesses. Too much security in the room. I'll take a cab there and back. I'll be perfectly safe." They stopped in front of the elevators.

He didn't look convinced and Meg knew she'd be wasting her breath if she kept on trying. Cruz had never been fond of situations where he didn't have complete control. Even knowing that, she was still surprised when he said, "I'm going with you."

He hated black-tie events. "No, you're not. You can't. You need a ticket."

The elevator doors opened and they were inside the empty space. It felt small and tight—even more so because Cruz was crowding her, his big body close. She moved back, stopping when her back hit the rear wall. He stayed where he was, giving her a little space.

"I *have* a ticket," he said. "I'll be sitting next to you at the head table."

She could feel her chest tightening up. "How did you manage that?"

Before he could answer, the elevator chimed and the doors opened. A young man and woman stepped inside. Cruz shifted slightly, putting himself between them and Meg.

Good grief. There wasn't a chance that she was going to be able to shake him. He didn't say anything until they got to their floor—just watched the other two passengers, who quite frankly, only appeared interested in each other.

When the elevator doors opened, he motioned for her to exit. He followed but didn't speak again until they were inside her room. "I called Beatrice Classen this morning. I wanted to talk to her about the four ex-cons that have worked at the hotel."

She gritted her teeth. "We discussed this."

"I know. And I didn't make any crazy accusations. I met with her and looked at the photos. Only two of the four were white. One of the two was a big guy, much taller and heavier than the person who pushed you. The other guy, Oscar Warren, was a possibility. No good alibi for last night but his time seems pretty well tied up for yesterday. He works at a food pantry."

"So, Oscar is off the hook?"

"Nobody is off the hook until we find the guy for sure. Let's just say that I'm moving on for right now."

She shook her head. "He didn't have a heart attack or anything when you started to question him?"

Cruz shook his head. "I was playing good cop. Used all my manners. Said please and thank-you."

She rolled her eyes. "So that still doesn't explain how you got a ticket for the event."

"I told Beatrice that I was your husband and that I wanted to surprise you."

"Ex-husband."

"Didn't have the same ring. I think she thought it was terribly romantic."

Beatrice was retired, after a thirty-year career

in bank management. Now she was devoting her time to A Hand Up. She'd also been married to the same man for her whole adult life. It stood to reason that she'd trip right over Cruz's story and fall in love with the whole idea.

Cruz gave her a light tap on the arm. "Better get dressed," he said.

She wanted to argue, maybe stomp her feet or bang her head against the wall. But she knew it wouldn't do any good. "Fine. We have to leave in thirty minutes," she said.

Twenty-nine minutes later she knocked on the adjoining door. She'd taken a shower, fixed her hair, put on fresh makeup and slipped into her new dress.

Cruz didn't answer the knock so she pushed the door open. The room was empty until Cruz walked out of the bathroom, playing with his tie.

Where is Waldo and what have you done with his cargo shorts?

Cruz wore a black tux, starched white shirt and burgundy cummerbund. His shoes were shined, his face shaved, and he smelled wonderful.

He looked so damn hot that she could feel vulnerable places tighten up in response. She felt unsteady and wondered if there was still time to raid the minibar.

He stared at her, his long, strong fingers still

holding the ends of his tie, his dark cop-eyes telling her nothing.

"I wasn't expecting this," she said. Her mouth felt dry and her brain was scrambled. She'd never seen Cruz in a tux. Even at their wedding, he'd opted for a dark suit. "I don't think you had that in your duffel bag."

He shook his head. "Got it this morning. Can you help me with this?"

No. It meant that she'd have to get even closer. His scent would linger with her, making her needy. She'd be squirming in her chair all night. It wasn't the kind of lasting impression she'd hoped to make on the crowd.

"Sure," she said. She took a deep breath before walking toward him. When they'd been married and he'd made detective, he'd complained relentlessly about having to wear a tie. She'd teased him that they almost managed to make him look civilized.

He'd begged for help and she'd become the resident expert. At night, he'd loosen the knot and slip the tie off, careful to make sure that all he needed to do for the next wear was reverse the steps. When it was time for the tie to be dry-cleaned, they did the whole routine all over again.

She reached for the silk and rubbed it gently between the tips of her index finger and thumb.

She heard his breath catch. His eyes were bright, his gaze intense.

Oh, Lordy. She needed to get control. Now. Or it might be never. She flipped one end over the other, threaded one through and tugged it tight. There. Done.

She stepped back so fast that she almost caught her dress in her heel. "We have to go," she said.

"Okay," he murmured. "You…ah…you're beautiful."

She stared at him. It would be so easy to slip back. It had been so long since she'd been held, loved. Wanted.

"I…I have something for you," he said. He walked over to his dresser and picked up a small gray box. He handed it to her.

She opened it. Inside, on plain white tissue paper, was a perfectly lovely sapphire necklace.

"I don't want you to feel obligated to wear it," he said. "It's just…I thought it would look nice with your eyes."

His voice was soft, uncertain. And she felt a piece of her already-damaged heart break off.

"It's lovely," she said. She lifted it out of the box, flipped open the catch, and put it on. It felt warm against her skin. She brushed the stone with the tips of her fingers.

"Thank you," she said. Her throat felt dry, her lips stiff.

"I was right," he said. "It's the same blue."

Another chunk of her heart broke off.

"I can't be late," she said and walked out the door.

Chapter Seven

The cab ride to the hotel was uneventful but Cruz could not shake the feeling that something bad was going to happen. It was no wonder. They were walking into an unsecured venue, with multiple access and egress points, and Meg, looking even more beautiful than usual, would be the center of attention. There would be lots of noise, lots of movement, lots of strangers.

In other words, a cluster of the most significant magnitude.

The driver made a sharp turn and pulled up close to the entrance. A uniformed doorman hustled over to open the door. Cruz didn't miss the appreciative glance that the man sent Meg's direction.

The smokers were milling around the entrance, puffing away their anxiety. Cruz wrapped an arm around Meg's shoulder, ignoring the startled look that she sent his direction. He guided her through the doors and across the lavish lobby.

There was a large poster advertising the event and a woman dressed in a long black dress with black gloves up to her elbows was waving people toward an elevator. "Fourth floor," she murmured.

In the elevator, Cruz maneuvered Meg into the corner and stood in front of her. The space was crowded—men in black tuxedoes, white shirts and ties. An occasional handkerchief in the pocket or brightly colored cummerbund around the waist was the only differentiation. Not so with the women. All colors of dresses, some to the floor, some to the knee, and one whose butt was barely covered. They wore lots of makeup and at least one of them smelled like burnt cinnamon toast.

The ballroom was straight ahead. Four sets of double doors were open and flanked on both sides by women in long dresses handing out programs. Before they had a chance to take a program, Beatrice Classen, wearing a long green dress and matching jacket trimmed with peacock feathers, swooped down upon them.

"Meg, Meg, this way. Oh, my, you look so lovely. Just like Annette Benning in that movie, you know, *The American President.*"

Cruz remembered the movie. He and Meg had only been married a year or so. It had been her turn to pick the movie and he'd made the obligatory groans and moans about watching a chick flick. But it had been worth it when Meg had agreed to watch it in bed and they'd had to DVR a portion of it to allow for a brief intermission of rainy afternoon sex.

He'd been fond of Annette Benning and Michael Douglas ever since.

Meg let the woman kiss her on both cheeks. Then she pulled back just a little and waved a hand in Cruz's direction. "Beatrice, Cruz Montoya. I understand you met this morning."

"Yes, yes. Nice to see you again, Mr. Montoya." Beatrice turned to Meg. "All this time and I never realized you were married."

"Cruz is actually my ex-husband," Meg said.

"Oh." Beatrice looked even more like a bird with her puckered mouth and furrowed forehead. "I'm…I'm…"

Cruz looked at Meg. *Now what?,* his eyes seemed to ask.

Cruz was probably right. It would be easier just to pass him off as her current husband. Easier tonight. But definitely more difficult the next time she met anyone from A Hand Up. They'd ask about her husband and at some point, she'd have to give the difficult explanation. *We're divorced. Have been for some time. Just friends now.*

She'd still be lying.

Meg put her arm around Beatrice's shoulders.

"It was really nice of you to be able to get him a ticket at such late notice. He's in town for just a short while."

"Happy to help," Beatrice said, her lined eyes full of speculation. But to her credit, she didn't probe. In her sixty-some years, she'd probably seen a lot of things. Maybe this wasn't that odd. "Let me show you to your seats," she said.

She led them through the large, dimly lit ballroom that was filled with round tables for ten. The overall effect of the starched linens, gleaming silverware, candles and flowers was stunning. Meg could feel her chest tighten up. This was a big deal. A Hand Up was an offshoot of one of the more high-profile charities in San Antonio. She really hoped she didn't screw up too badly.

Beatrice pointed to a chair. "Here we are."

Place cards were already at the table. *Meg Montoya. Cruz Montoya.* Silver script on a pale blue background. Almost seven years earlier, there'd been very similar cards. The room had been smaller, the tables less lavish, but there had been laughter and love and great anticipation.

At their wedding.

When she'd been packing to leave Chicago, she'd come across the place cards. Unable to destroy them, unable to leave them, she'd stuffed them into the side pocket of her suitcase. When she'd arrived in San Antonio, she'd left them there. Sort of the same way all her things from her office in Chicago had been left in a box when she'd arrived in San Antonio. She couldn't bear to part with them, nor could she bear the daily reminders of the life she'd left behind.

Her spot was next to the podium, with Cruz to her right. There were three more chairs on their side and on the other side of the podium, a matching five. Ten spots at the head table. Places for Beatrice and her husband as well as for the other three directors of A Hand Up and their guests.

A cocktail server approached with a tray of champagne glasses. Meg took one, Cruz shook his head. She sipped and glanced around the room. "Big place," she said.

"I think that's what I tried to tell you," Cruz agreed. He was scanning the room.

"Got the exits identified?" she asked. Since their very first date, the pattern had been established. They'd go to dinner, a movie, heck, even the zoo. Cruz would choose his chair or spot with care. He'd have at least a couple escape routes in his head. Just in case there was fire, flood…locusts.

She'd teased him that he was ready for everything but nuclear fallout. But secretly she'd appreciated his common sense. She had always felt safe with Cruz.

The other directors arrived and Meg shook hands and made introductions. She kept it simple. "This is Cruz. He's visiting from Chicago." Then it was time to eat.

And Cruz, being Cruz, caused just a minor disturbance when the servers tried to deliver their plates. He shook his head when the server tried to give Meg her dinner. "We'll take two off that tray," he said, pointing at a tray that another server was carrying. The young man looked at him, started to protest, then apparently recalled the part of his training that said the customer is always right. He nodded and fetched two plates from the other tray.

Meg figured the waitstaff would be talking about them for weeks. Making jokes about the weird things people did. "I really don't think there is somebody in the kitchen trying to poison me," she whispered.

Cruz simply shrugged and buttered his roll.

The chicken might have been delicious. But Meg was too nervous to really taste it. She cut it and her roasted potatoes and asparagus into teeny bites and ate a little but mostly pushed the rest around her plate until she gave up altogether. Public speaking always made her nervous but she'd gotten used to it. For many years now, she'd been regularly speaking at shareholder events or at employee meetings.

But this was different.

These people were strangers and they'd paid five hundred bucks a plate to hear her. Plus, she didn't want to make a fool of herself in front of Charlotte and Scott and the other staff who rounded out the BJM table. As promised, they were near the front. Charlotte wore a beautiful silver gown and Scott, like Cruz, had on a tux.

He looked…nice. Not hot and alpha like Cruz who seemed to simply *own* his space. Scott was polished, sophisticated. And that certainly wasn't bad. He and Charlotte had arrived late, just as the salads were brought out. She knew Cruz had seen them arrive. Heck, the man saw everything. But he didn't say anything and didn't acknowledge the table.

He hadn't talked to her during dinner, either. But once the server cleared her plate, he leaned over and whispered in her ear, "Calm down. You're going to do great."

"This could be a disaster," she whispered back.

A disaster. Yeah. Maybe so. He wasn't worried about Meg's speech or her ability to deliver it. She'd always underestimated herself while he'd always known just how smart and talented she was.

He probably should have tried to talk her off the ledge during dinner. But while he'd made it appear as if his greatest interest in the world was a piece of chicken that could have used some salt, he'd been busy studying the room.

They'd whipped the place into shape. It looked way different than it had earlier this morning. They had dimmed the lighting slightly, making it more intimate. It also made it more difficult for him to see more than a hundred yards out. Even so, he still had a view of the tables he was most interested in. He figured if somebody intended to harm Meg, they'd have a spot near the front because the logical points of escape were the side doors on the left and right side of the room.

Meg was right. He had checked out the doors when he'd been here earlier. The rear doors led to the lobby. If anyone tried to escape that way, too many people would see or maybe even try to apprehend him.

The side door on the left led to a hallway that led to the kitchen. There were stairs midway that led to a street-level exit. The side door on the right led to a bank of elevators that went up twenty floors to guest rooms. If someone had a good head start in either direction, they'd be hard to find.

What he saw when he looked around the dining room didn't concern him too much. When Meg had left his room earlier to get dressed, he'd taken five minutes to review the photos of all the employees who'd been termed by BJM Hotels within the past year. None of the faces at the tables looked familiar. Of course, now he was looking at the backs of a whole lot of heads. Once the program began, he figured people would turn their chairs and he'd get a look at their faces.

Waitstaff came around with dessert. Meg declined and the server, proving he was a fast study, allowed Cruz to pick one off a tray. It was angel food cake, strawberries and whipped cream, layered in a tall glass. The presentation was nice and it tasted significantly better than the chicken.

Then Beatrice pushed her chair back and came up to the podium. She was so short that she had to pull down the adjustable microphone or it would have conked her in the forehead.

"Thank you so much for coming. You've demonstrated a great commitment to A Hand Up. When we contemplated this program a few years ago..."

Blah, blah, blah. Cruz kept his eyes moving, watching the crowd. He'd been right. The people with their backs to the stage were turning their chairs. He scanned the room and didn't see anything that worried him.

Saw a bunch of things that annoyed him, though. People were checking their phones and a few were chatting to the person next to them. A couple even had their eyes closed, taking a short snooze. Idiots. They'd dropped serious change to be here and they couldn't even pretend to be interested.

His dear mother would have smacked them up alongside their heads. *Be respectful.* She'd drilled it into her children's heads. If somebody is talking to you, be quiet and listen. If someone older comes into the room, get up and give him your seat. If you can hold the door for someone, do it.

He hadn't always embraced the lessons. In Chicago, especially on the south side of the city, kids grew up quick. At ten, he'd been a troublemaker. At eleven, a punk. At twelve, on the fast track to juvie. His mother had worried and pleaded and prayed. His father had yelled and drank and yelled some more.

Then he'd left.

And life got even harder for the Montoyas. If not for his mom, and the strength of both her character and her back, as she worked twelve-hour days cleaning hotel rooms, he might well have ended up on the wrong side of a jail cell, like the young men in this room who either had been or were currently clients of A Hand Up.

"...a great honor to introduce a wonderful partner to A Hand Up. She is a woman who understands the importance of giving others purpose. She has the rare ability to encourage others to reach for the stars while making sure that the ladder they're standing on is nice and steady. Ladies and gentlemen, please help me welcome Meg Montoya."

Meg pushed her chair back. He wanted to squeeze her hand or pat her back—something to reassure her. He kept his hands down. Those days were gone. Now, a touch, his touch, would just throw her off her stride.

"Good evening. It's a pleasure to be here. It has been my privilege to partner with A Hand Up to give hardworking individuals an opportunity for a better future. I first became…"

Her voice was strong, confident, and he could see people in the audience responding. Phones got put down, side conversations ceased, people listened.

"…and while I hope that the program participants benefited, I know with great certainly that BJM Hotels is better for having had the opportunity to work with these four individuals. Michael worked in our purchasing department and he…"

Cruz heard the scrape of a nearby chair. He turned his head slightly and from the left side of the room, a man was running toward the stage, his eyes fixated on Meg. He was young, white and had one arm raised, like an Olympic torch bearer.

There was no torch, no flame—just the glint of a steel blade from a dangerous-looking knife.

Chapter Eight

Cruz shoved his chair aside. "Get back," he yelled at Meg. He jumped up onto the table, sending dishes and glasses flying, and leapt toward the man who was less than ten feet away.

He knocked the man to the ground, they rolled, and in seconds, Cruz had the idiot facedown, spread-eagle, with the knife safely secured under the heel of his shoe.

People were screaming, running from the room. He ignored it all. Just turned his head to make sure that Meg was okay.

She was back at the microphone. "Ladies and gentlemen. Please return to your seats. For the safety of everyone, sit down and remain calm. There is no danger. Everything is fine."

Her voice was not as steady as before but it did the trick. People stopped screaming. They sat down. Order resumed.

Two male security officers arrived, looking

slightly green. Cruz figured they probably hadn't had much experience handling knife-wielding maniacs.

Fortunately or unfortunately for him, he'd had his share of experience. But never before had he been so absolutely terrified. He'd looked into the man's eyes, realized Meg was the intended target and his heart had about stopped.

"Police are on the way," the younger security officer said.

"Thank you," said the other. "This could have been bad."

It could have been horrific. He could have lost Meg forever.

Four San Antonio police officers arrived. Cruz identified himself, gave a brief recap of what had happened and stepped back, grateful to let them take over. He wanted to stand next to Meg, smell her rich scent, hear her sweet laugh.

But that was going to have to wait. Meg, always the consummate professional, asked the police if she could give her statement once the program was concluded. The cops agreed. So after bagging the knife, they quietly escorted the man from the room. Cruz saw one of the officers pause at the table where the man had been sitting and exchange a few words before leaving the room. The door was barely closed behind them when Meg launched back into her speech. She kept it short but gave a brief description of the contributions from each of the four individuals from A Hand Up. Each man was asked to stand. Cruz noted that Oscar Warren didn't even look in his direction.

Finally, there was applause and closing remarks from Beatrice Classen and the event was over.

It had been the longest ten minutes of his life, full of frustration. He desperately wanted five minutes alone with the attacker but knew the San Antonio police weren't going to let that happen. Professional courtesy only got a person so far. They'd be crossing a line if they let him get too close to the investigation.

He wanted Meg away from the ugliness. Didn't want her goodness soiled by the tediousness of what needed to happen next. The police would have questions, maybe even the press, depending on whether it was a slow news day or not.

The people at the attacker's table remained seated. Cruz figured the cop had told them to hang out after the program ended. Even if the man had acted alone, he may have engaged in some dinner conversation that would help the police with their investigation.

The rest of the attendees were bookin' it toward the doors at the rear. Unfortunately, Slater and

Charlotte were swimming upstream, headed toward Meg.

"Gracious, Meg," said Charlotte. "That was certainly unexpected."

Cruz gave the woman a look. Her tone was almost chiding, like it was somehow Meg's fault. But Meg didn't seem to notice.

"Well, the good news is I imagine I won't have to worry about being next year's keynote speaker," Meg said. She was working hard to keep it light but Cruz knew her too well. She was shook.

"Do any of you know him?" Cruz asked.

Meg, Slater and Charlotte all shook their heads. Slater put his hand on Meg's arm. Cruz balled his fist, desperately wanting to knock him back a step.

"I sure hope this ends all the craziness," Slater said. "He's got to be the guy behind the letters and the damage to your car and your apartment."

"I imagine he is," Meg said. "I mean, how many people could hate me?" She smiled, still trying to keep the mood light.

"Charlotte mentioned getting a nightcap. Can you join us?" Slater asked.

"I'm sure the police are going to want to talk to her," Charlotte said. "She can't just go running out of here."

Charlotte was right. But it wasn't as if Meg was the type to run away from her responsibilities.

Meg didn't seem to take offense, however. "You're right, Charlotte," she said. "Please, go without me. Who knows how long this will take?"

IT TOOK ANOTHER ninety minutes. By the time Meg finished giving the police her statement, the wait-staff had gone home. The tables were completely stripped with the exception of a few rogue salt shakers. Dirty linens were piled in one corner of the room and chairs stacked in the other.

They'd had question after question but she hadn't been able to tell them much. All she could remember was the panic. Hers. When she'd heard Cruz's shout to get back, she'd turned her head, only to see him jump up onto the table to face a knife-wielding maniac.

He hadn't hesitated. Not for a second.

He'd saved her life. And maybe others, too.

"Thank you," she said. It was inadequate but she felt compelled to say something once they finally got cleared to go. They waited for the elevator. It was the first time they'd been alone since the event had occurred.

"I'm sorry," he said. "I was hoping this was over."

"Me, too." The enormity of the situation had hit her hard about fifteen minutes earlier when Detective Myers, who had been called in, had confided that they weren't confident that the attacker had anything to do with the threats she'd received or the damage to her car or house. The attacker had denied it and seemed to have an alibi that would hold up.

Myers had explained that the man had hidden in the hotel for hours and during the confusion of everyone entering the ballroom, had come in through a side door. He'd taken a seat at a table that had an open chair and acted as if he had every right to be there.

Cruz had listened to the detective's explanation and his jaw had gotten so tight that she was surprised it hadn't cracked. Now, he simply looked as if he were simmering, about to boil over.

"Want to get a drink?" she asked.

He raised an eyebrow. She understood. She hadn't exactly been extending the olive branch lately. But the very last thing she wanted was to go back to her hotel room and go to bed, only to stare at the white ceiling and think about all of this for one more minute.

She wanted to forget it. Forget everything. Just forget. "This hotel has a nice bar in the lower level."

"I guess I wouldn't turn down a beer."

Five minutes later, they slid into a corner booth. The room was dark, a little noisy, offering just the right insulation from the rest of the world. She considered the wine list but ordered a margarita instead. It came in a pretty glass with salt on the rim and tasted so good. When she ordered her second, Cruz asked for some chips and salsa, too.

Five minutes later, he pushed the chip bowl toward her and pulled her drink away. "You might want to slow down a little," he said. She shook her head, reached for her drink and took another big swallow.

"Want to talk about it?" he asked.

"Not really," she said. Now she did reach for the chips. He couldn't expect her to spill her guts if her mouth was full. If she didn't want to think about it, then she sure as heck didn't want to *talk* about it.

The salsa was gone and almost all the chips by the time the waitress swung back around for the third time. Meg pointed to her glass and smiled.

"We ought to go," Cruz said.

The waitress paused, looked from one to another.

"Not yet," Meg said.

Cruz shook his head and motioned for another beer. "I hate to see a lady drink alone," he said, just as soon as the waitress was out of hearing distance.

By the time Meg finished her third margarita, her cheeks were feeling numb and she was pleasantly relaxed. And she wasn't thinking of anything. Well, that wasn't exactly true. She was thinking of how handsome Cruz was. And nice. Patient.

She wasn't a drinker. He knew that. But he also seemed to understand that she needed to numb her mind. He wasn't lecturing or chiding, he was simply sitting back, nursing his own beers.

"I suppose we should go," she said.

"Okay." He stood up. She did the same. When she swayed just a little, Cruz cupped her elbow with his hand. He motioned to the waitress who hurried over with the check. Cruz looked at it briefly, threw some bills on the table and guided her toward the door.

"I'm fine," she said.

"Sure you are," he said. He held up an arm to flag down a cab. "We probably should walk it off but until this guy is caught, I don't like the idea of you being in the open. Too many nooks and crannies for the crazies to hide in."

Meg slid into the cab and closed her eyes. She was so tired. It seemed as if she hadn't slept in days. When they got to the front door of her hotel, she forced herself to perk up. Security watched the entrances 24/7 and she didn't want it circulating through the break room that she'd dragged herself in, looking like death warmed over.

The absurdity of it hit her, almost making her stumble. A man with a knife had almost attacked her. She had a right to be a little upset, didn't she? But no. She wanted everyone to think she was *just fine*.

Because she always wanted everyone to think everything was just fine.

When nothing had really been fine for a long time.

She stood in the empty hallway while Cruz quickly checked both their rooms. When he motioned that she could enter, she sank into a corner chair, dropping her purse next to her feet. She slipped off the heels that were starting to hurt.

"You should get some sleep," Cruz said. He remained near the door, his stance alert.

"I want another drink," she said.

He shook his head.

"I'm a big girl, Cruz. I can have another drink if I want it." She knew she sounded childish.

He didn't respond. Just moved slowly over to the bed and sat down at the end. He removed his own shoes, his necktie and cummerbund and lay back. He folded his arms, propped them under his head like a pillow, and closed his eyes. "Drink away," he said. "Just don't leave the room."

There wasn't much chance of that. She'd slept with Cruz for six years. The man could hear a pin drop. She'd turn the doorknob and he'd have her spread-eagle, smelling the carpet.

"Not to worry," she mumbled. She opened the minibar, peered at the contents, once again considered the red wine, but decided on a beer. She figured it would mix better with the margaritas. Instead of chips, there were peanuts.

She sat back in her chair, nursed her beer, nibbled on the peanuts and studied Cruz.

He was so darn handsome. He'd inherited his mother's high cheekbones and her smooth, mocha skin tone. His thick, dark hair wasn't silky—no that was too feminine of a word. It was...*smooth, sensual.* When they were open, his dark eyes were wise, having seen all kinds of bad and good in the world.

She'd never meet anyone like him again. She'd never love anyone like she'd loved him.

Pain squeezed her middle, making it hard to breathe.

She'd given him up. Had walked away and tried not to look back. Had faced the knowledge that one day she'd stumble across him on Facebook, with one arm around his wife, the other cradling his children. And she'd think about sending him a message.

So happy you moved on.

Chapter Thirty-Two of the Big Lie.

But fate had intervened and now he was lying on her bed. And she didn't want to be reasonable or pragmatic or even kind.

She wanted to be carefree and spontaneous and maybe even a little selfish. She set her unfinished beer on the floor and stood up. She unzipped her dress, slipped her arms out and let the gown fall to the floor.

For several minutes she stood perfectly still, in panties and a strapless bra, watching Cruz. He hadn't moved. His breathing hadn't changed.

And she almost chickened out.

But she wanted him with a desperation that bordered on insanity.

She unsnapped her bra, took off her panties and stepped over her discarded clothes. She approached the bed and reached for the buckle on his belt.

Chapter Nine

Cruz grabbed her wrist and opened his eyes. Her face was pale, her eyes big and her sweet lips were pressed together in fierce concentration. "What the hell are you doing?" he snarled.

He'd been a wreck since he'd heard her stand up and unzip her dress. He'd waited, expecting her to go to her room. Had been prepared to spend another night thinking about her, dreaming about what it would be like to hold her again, to slip inside her.

Then he'd heard the soft sound of the material hitting the carpet and knew that she was almost naked.

It was a miracle his own zipper had held up.

She stared at him. "I want to have sex with you," she said finally.

Yes. Yes. A thousand times yes. "You've had too much to drink, Meg. Go to bed." He let go of her wrist and scooted farther up on the mattress, away from her.

"I'm not drunk, Cruz. I know what I'm doing."

She straightened up and stood before him. And damn it, he looked. Like a condemned man staring at his last days of freedom, he drank in the sight.

Breasts, firm yet so soft with pale pink nipples. High ribs, slim waist, narrow hips. So feminine with her long legs and pale skin that had freckles in the most interesting places.

He felt hot and edgy and he clenched and unclenched his hand to release some of the tension. "This isn't a game you're playing, Meg."

She put a knee on the bed.

"Look," he said. "I appreciate the offer but—"

Other knee on the bed. Less than a foot separated them. She was killing him.

She reached out, letting her fingers dance across his thigh, then higher. Her fingers rested on the thin material of his tuxedo pants. Then she gently stroked the length of him.

He wanted to push himself into her hand, her mouth. He wanted to roll her underneath him and not stop until one of them passed out.

But he kept still. Somehow.

"Please?" she asked.

Damn. He'd never been able to refuse her anything. And he sure as hell wasn't going to start tonight.

He sat up, cupped one hand around the back of

her head and pulled her close. And he kissed her. Softly, at first. Then she opened her mouth and drew him in.

So familiar. So new.

He shifted, pulling her down next to him. Her skin was warm and he could smell the sweet scent of her wanting him. "Last chance to walk away," he whispered, his tone deliberately light.

She shook her head. And when she reached for his belt this time, he didn't stop her.

Meg woke up when Cruz's cell phone rang. She glanced at the clock next to the bed and was surprised to see that it was almost 9:00 a.m. She never slept that late, even on the weekends.

She hadn't gotten all that much sleep. She and Cruz had made love three times. The first time had been frenzied, both of them so needy that it seemed as if they would inhale each other. The second and third times had been different. No less passion, no smaller fireworks, but still calmer, more soothing, more sensual.

There wasn't a spot on her body that he hadn't touched, kissed, loved. The man had always been an energetic lover but last night he'd seemed driven to take her to new heights.

And she'd been happy to go there. Had been delighted to see his response to her touch, had felt the desire tear through her when she'd known his release was near.

Now he had his big body curled around her, her back to his front. And by the feel of things, he was ready for round four.

"Are you going to answer that?" she asked.

He reached his arm out to the bedside table and picked up his cell phone to peer at the number. "It's my sister," he mumbled. "I'll call her back."

She scooted away. "Take it. I have to pee anyway."

When she came back to the bed, he was still on the phone. He'd moved and was sitting up, a pen in his hand, a hotel notepad resting on the blanket that covered him. He was smiling, looking slightly amused.

"Congratulations," he said. "I always thought you were a pit bull. Those other sales reps didn't have a chance." He listened, then glanced at Meg. His voice got more serious. "I'm not exactly here on a vacation," he said. "I'm…helping Meg."

She sat down on the bed. "What's going on?" she whispered.

"Hang on, sis." He held the phone up against his chest. "My sister won a sales contest. It's a trip to Las Vegas. It's this weekend. Her husband is out of town on a business trip. She had a babysitter lined up but the woman has the flu. So she doesn't have anybody to watch her little girl."

"Oh." Meg could feel her heart rate accelerate. Elsa didn't have any other family in Texas. "You should do it," she said.

"Are you sure?" he asked. "We're not any closer to finding the creep who's been hassling you."

"Maybe because he's not any closer to me. Maybe he's had his fun and he's moved on to his next victim."

He hesitated and then put the phone back to his ear. "As usual your big brother can bail you out. Drop off the rug rat anytime. I'll have her tossing back shots by noon."

He listened, laughed and said goodbye. When he clicked the end button, he was shaking his head.

"This should be fun," he said. "Where should we take her for lunch?"

We. Elsa's little girl would be almost four, twice the age of Missy when she'd died.

Meg could feel her chest pull even tighter. She felt light-headed, almost dizzy.

She couldn't help Cruz. She couldn't watch over a child. She just couldn't.

"I…I have to work, Cruz. There's no way I can help you."

He cocked his head. "You have to work all weekend?" he asked, his tone puzzled but still pleasant.

"Yes. Yes, I do. Scott gave me a special project. I don't want to disappoint him."

She could see the muscles in Cruz's jaw tighten. "I'm not trying to get in the way of your work, Meg. But I thought we might spend some time together. Especially after last night."

He sounded so wounded that she almost caved. But if he knew about the past, he'd realize that both he and his niece were better off without her.

"Last night was…nice. But it didn't change anything."

"Nice?" He threw off the blanket, grabbed his briefs off the floor and yanked them on. Then he started to pace around the room. "Are you kidding me?" He ran his hands through his hair, making it stand on end. "Nice?" His voice was louder, harsher. "Thanks for the time in the sack, Cruz. I had an itch and you scratched it so very *nicely.* Now, I'm good to go for another year or so—" he threw her a look that could kill "—or until I get up close and friendly with my boss."

She felt stiff and old and so brittle that if she bumped into anything little pieces would fall off. With as much dignity as she could, given that she was still naked, she gathered up her discarded clothes from the night before and walked over to the connecting door. She paused, her back to him.

Without turning she said, "For what it's worth, Cruz, I'm sorry. I didn't mean to hurt you."

Then she walked into her room, dumped her clothes in a pile, stepped into the shower and started to cry.

Chapter Ten

Cruz stood in the lobby of the hotel and drank his coffee. It was hot and strong, just the way he liked it. But there was nothing that could take away the bitter taste in his mouth.

He'd been a damn idiot. Had opened up the playbook and read something into last night that wasn't on the page. All Meg had been looking for was a few hours of hot sex. She'd tried to drink her way to oblivion but when that didn't work, she'd decided to screw her way to it.

He crushed his now-empty paper cup. He wanted to hate her for it. At the very least, he wanted to be able to walk away from her.

But he couldn't do either. It wasn't her fault that he'd made it more than it was. She hadn't promised anything. Certainly hadn't pledged her love. Had simply gone for his belt buckle and he'd been happy to let her nimble fingers and other equally pliant parts do their thing.

Just sex. That's all it was.

Amazing sex. So good that after she went to her room to shower, he'd gone from being so angry that the top of his head might blow off to thinking that maybe once a year was enough. He'd finished getting dressed, then stepped out into the empty hallway to wait for in-house security to arrive. All the while debating the merits of an arrangement where they would meet at an off-the-grid spot, screw each other blind and go about their merry way until the next year.

He thought he'd seen an old movie with a similar story line. But damned if he could remember if there'd been a happy ending.

When Tim Burtiss had gotten off the elevator, Cruz had filled him in quickly. While Meg wasn't necessarily in any more danger than she had been the night before, the attack at the dinner was too fresh in his mind. It appeared to be absolutely unrelated but in his gut he felt as if things were close to coming to a head.

He'd advised the security guard that Meg was getting dressed and intended to go to her office. The young man promised to stick with her until she returned to the room at the end of the day.

Now Cruz dropped his mangled coffee cup into the fancy trash container and was considering buying another cup when he saw his sister pull up. He went outside to help her with Jana.

"Morning, Cruz," Elsa said, giving him a hard hug and a quick kiss on the cheek.

"Hey, sis. You're looking good," he added.

"Oh, thanks. This is my 'harried mother, forgot her favorite book' look."

Cruz laughed and opened up Jana's door. She was in a car seat, belted in like an astronaut. He was shocked to see how big she was. Granted, it had been more than a year since he'd seen her.

"Hey, darling, remember Uncle Cruz?"

She stared at him with big brown eyes.

"Your mom is on her way to spend your inheritance so you're going to hang out with me," he said. "I have a reputation for being very good with four-year-old women."

She wasn't crying but there weren't any smiles coming his way. She did let him unbuckle her car seat and accepted his hand as he helped her crawl out of the car.

Elsa knelt down before her. "You're going to stay with Uncle Cruz for two nights. Then I'll be back to pick you up. You'll be a good girl for him, won't you?"

Jana nodded and Elsa gave her a quick, hard hug. When his sister stood up, there were tears in her eyes.

"I've got this, sis," Cruz said. "It'll be fine."

"I know. It's just hard to leave her." Elsa looked around. "Where's Meg?"

"Working," Cruz said, trying to keep the tone light.

She studied him. "I don't know what's going on here, Cruz, but please don't get hurt again. A year ago I wasn't sure you'd bounce back."

"Don't worry about me. I'm tougher than I look," he added.

She frowned at him. Then gave her daughter one more quick hug and got in the car without another word. Jana watched her drive away, still not saying anything.

Cruz felt about as competent as a rookie at his first domestic disturbance. He stuck his hands in his pockets. "Are you hungry?" he asked.

She nodded.

"There's a McDonald's two blocks away."

For the first time, she smiled. He held out his hand and she took it. "I like pancakes," she announced.

"Coming right up," he said.

MEG PUSHED PAPERS around on her desk for the first hour. Yes, she had work to do. She always did. But there wasn't anything that couldn't have waited until Monday. There was no special project that Scott needed help with.

She wondered what Cruz and Jana were doing? Cruz didn't know the area well. The least she could have done is taken a few minutes to get him acclimated. But she'd been so focused on her own panic that she hadn't been able to think of anything else.

Tonight she'd make an effort to be a little more helpful. She could make him a list of kid-friendly locations. She'd done the same for lots of other guests.

Although he was clearly getting perks that not every guest had access to.

She put her head in her hands. How could she have been so stupid? She'd slept with him. Not that there'd been much sleeping. Just a bunch of orgasms and other good stuff. Like having her hair stroked. And the insides of her thighs kissed. And her heart squeezed when she'd looked up and he had his head thrown back, the veins in his neck tight, as he poured himself into her.

Well, sort of. Luckily, he'd had some condoms in his travel bag. It had been touch and go for a minute the first time. Things had escalated quickly and suddenly he'd been inside her. She had enough sense to choke out that she wasn't on the Pill any longer. He'd stared at her, a thousand questions in his dark eyes. But somehow he'd had the good sense not to ask any of them. Instead, he'd got suited up and they'd continued on, without missing a beat.

If his sister hadn't called, they might still be in bed. They would have had to call for nourishment and some more condoms.

The irony did not escape her. She'd been afraid to walk into the hotel looking tipsy yet she'd have been perfectly fine letting the front desk know that she was in need of birth control. Post haste.

Her brain had exploded. Either before, during or after one of those fabulous orgasms. That could be the only explanation.

It wasn't much of an excuse but it was the best she had.

She wanted to blame it on the alcohol. She'd drunk too much. No debate there. But she hadn't been too drunk to know what she was doing. She'd sat in the chair, nursed her beer and thought about what-ifs. What if Cruz hadn't stopped the man? What if she'd been stabbed? What if Cruz had been hurt? What if he'd been killed?

It had suddenly been too much. And the only thing that could make it better was a couple of hours in his arms.

And then morning had come as it inevitably did. When his sister had called, it had been clear that he wanted to help her out, that he wanted to spend time with his niece. And Meg wasn't going to stand in his way. She'd made that decision twelve months ago. There was no need to go back and revisit it.

Cruz Montoya was a good man. She wanted him to be happy. To have a houseful of kids. To have a wife who wasn't damaged by her own past. He deserved to be able to trust the mother of his children. He should never have to worry if his children were safe.

And if he ever found out what she'd done, he'd never stop worrying.

CRUZ HAD BEEN happy enough to eat breakfast at McDonald's and hadn't really even minded when Jana had insisted upon eating lunch there, too. She almost had him talked into a third trip for chocolate chip cookies when he felt the imaginary hot scorch of his sister's disapproval square between his shoulder blades.

Instead, he steered his rental car into the parking lot of a small grocery store where he bought a bunch of bananas, a package of grapes and a quart of milk—he figured if Jana didn't drink it all, he could shove the remainder into the minibar. After all, Meg had emptied a couple shelves the night before.

She wasn't on birth control. What the hell did that mean? She'd always faithfully taken the Pill while they'd been married. Was she leaving it to Slater? Was he sterile? Was she trying to get pregnant?

Was it even possible that she and Slater weren't having sex? His mind had whirled with unanswered questions all day.

"Now where are we going?" Jana asked, skipping alongside him.

They'd spent the morning at the aquarium and the afternoon at Kiddie Park. "Back to the hotel to watch movies. Uncle Cruz is exhausted."

"I'm not tired," she said.

"Of course not," he said.

They were still a couple miles from the hotel when he saw something that made him do a double take. Charlotte. Walking down the street, hanging all over some guy.

Cruz took another look and almost ran into the car in front of him that had stopped for a red light.

Mason Hawkins. The man was Mason Hawkins. He'd put on some pants, washed his hair and ditched the potato chips.

They were deep in conversation and Charlotte reached up to touch the man's face. Cruz wanted to jump out of the car and demand to know what the hell was going on. But he had Jana and the light was changing. He pressed on the gas.

Ten minutes later, he and Jana were back in the

room. He took off her shoes, washed the grime of the day from her face and hands, and had her crawl up onto the bed. He made her comfortable with some pillows and then they flipped through the in-room movie channel until she picked one about a dolphin that didn't have a tail. He pressed Select and settled back against his own pillows, strangely content to be watching a kid-friendly movie.

Fifteen minutes later he heard a card slide into the door's electronic lock. Meg walked in the room. She looked tired. Beautiful, but tired.

Officer Burtiss stood in the doorway. "Same time tomorrow, Meg?" he asked.

She nodded. "That would be great."

He looked at Cruz. "Will you need me anymore tonight, sir?"

Cruz looked at Meg. She shook her head. "No, that should do it," he said. "Thank you."

Officer Burtiss stepped back into the hallway and closed the door. Meg kicked off her shoes, set her briefcase and purse on the floor and sank into the chair in the corner of the room. She smiled in Jana's direction.

"How long has she been sleeping?"

"Since about thirty seconds after we started the movie. Of course, she wasn't tired."

"Did you find your way around the city okay? I probably should have made a couple suggestions."

No, she probably should have come with. Then he could have solely focused on the day rather than his attention being splintered between watching and enjoying Jana and worrying like hell about Meg. He was still mad about her abrupt insistence that she had to work. "I think the hotel has a concierge for that, don't they?"

She started to respond, stopped and said nothing. Now her tired eyes were filled with hurt. It didn't make him feel any better that she'd gotten the point. "Never mind," he said, waving his hand. "Anything new happen today?"

She shook her head. "I'm going to take a shower."

She was in the doorway, between their rooms, when he remembered what he'd seen. "I saw Charlotte today," he said. "She was with Mason Hawkins."

Meg frowned. "My Charlotte?"

He nodded. "You hadn't mentioned that there was a relationship there."

"Because I didn't know there was one. Are you sure?"

He nodded. "It's weird because I got the feeling the other night at the dinner that she might have a thing for Slater."

Now Meg was shaking her head, as if it was too much to take in. "I think she admires Scott. We all do for what he's been able to do with the hotel."

Cruz rolled his eyes.

Meg ignored him. "But she certainly never said anything about Hawkins. I guess I do recall a couple times that I walked into the office and he was there but she always had some excuse. He was dropping off invoices for me to sign. We'd sent up a check request without a signature. Things that made sense to me."

"When he lost his job, she didn't say anything? Didn't try to plead his case?"

Meg shook her head. "No, but there is something that suddenly makes more sense, though. When we terminate an employee because of their misconduct, we protest their unemployment claim. This saves the hotel money. And most of the time, we win. But we didn't win his and when we investigated why, we learned that our protest never reached them. It never got faxed in. Charlotte was responsible for making sure that happened. I didn't think too much about it. She handles a huge workload and every once in a while, something is going to fall through the cracks."

"Now that you know, do you intend to say something to her?"

"I don't know. I need to think about it."

He nodded and she left the room. He leaned back against his pillows and closed his eyes. An hour later, Jana stirred. She opened her big brown eyes, arched her back like a cat, gave him a sweet smile and slid off the bed. "I'm hungry," she said.

He was, too. It had been more than six hours since lunch. He got up, poured Jana a glass of milk and grabbed a banana. He turned to hand it to her and realized that she'd spied the barely open door to Meg's room and had made tracks.

He poked his head around the door. Meg was lying on the bed. There was an open book next to her. Jana had crawled up and was sitting next to her, Indian-style. She was leaning forward, studying Meg, who was perfectly still, sort of like a deer caught in headlights.

"So do you *live* here?" Jana asked. "This is the nicest house I've ever seen."

"I work here at the hotel. I'm staying for just a few days."

"Mama said that you used to be Uncle Cruz's wife."

Meg swallowed. "That's right. I knew you when you were born," she added.

"How come you're not married anymore?" Jana asked.

Cruz felt his chest tighten up. *Yeah, Meg. How come?*

"I…" Meg's eyes lifted, resting on him. She pressed her lips together. "Grown-up reasons, Jana."

Jana pointed at Meg's hands. "You have pretty nails. Can you paint mine?" she asked.

Meg smiled. "I could probably do that. As long as it's okay with your uncle."

"Fingers. Toes. Knock yourselves out," Cruz said, grateful that the little girl had moved on to other topics. Meg had left him because she didn't love him anymore. That's what she'd told him a year ago and based on her actions this morning, nothing much had changed.

He put Jana's snack on the table next to the bed. "Jana and I were thinking dinner sounded good. Would you mind if we ordered in?"

"I want macaroni and cheese," Jana piped in.

Meg smiled. This time it reached her eyes. "I think the kitchen can manage that," she said. "I'll have the salmon."

Cruz rounded out the order with a steak, wine for Meg and a beer for himself. Then he shaved and jumped in the shower. He had just finished dressing when there was a knock on his door.

"Room service."

Cruz looked through the peephole. There was a young woman on the other side, holding a tray. He slipped his gun into the small of his back before carefully opening the door.

"Hi," he said. "You can just put it there." He motioned to the table closest to the door. Once she had the table set, he scrawled his name on the charge slip. She wished him good-night and left. He locked the door behind her, then poked his head around the connecting door.

Jana was still next to Meg. The little girl was on her back, her arms stretched out like a zombie and her feet flexed, evidently so that she could admire her freshly painted fingernails and toenails. Meg was sitting up, bent over her leg, touching up the polish on her own toes.

They looked…perfect. Connected. Their dark hair was almost the same shade. They could have been mother and daughter.

Cruz felt the burn in his chest. Someday Meg would have someone else's child.

"Cruz?" Meg lifted her head. "Did you say something?"

Damn. Had he done something extraordinarily unmanly like moan? "Dinner's here," he said.

Jana scrambled off the bed. "Yeah, is there ice cream?"

"Only if you eat your carrots," Cruz said.

She stopped in her tracks. "Carrots," she repeated.

Cruz nodded. "It's chocolate ice cream."

The little girl scrunched up her face. "How many carrots?"

"How old are you?" Cruz asked.

"Four."

"Then five. You always want to be one carrot ahead."

She considered, then smiled, showing her small, white teeth. "You've got a deal, Uncle Cruz."

They pulled their chairs around the small table in the lower half of Cruz's room. He opened the sliding glass door but kept the vertical blinds mostly closed. The sounds of the River Walk, rich with early-evening laughter and chatter, drifted in. Latin music was playing somewhere.

Meg took a sip of her wine and felt herself relax for the first time that day. She'd just lifted her glass for a second sip when her cell phone buzzed. She picked it up, recognized the number as Sanjoi from in-house security, and answered.

She listened, then very carefully put her glass down. By the time the call ended, she felt cold all over.

"Meg?" Cruz asked, already standing.

"Someone broke into my office and the damage is extensive," she said, repeating what she'd heard. She lifted her head. "There's blood. Smeared across my desk."

Chapter Eleven

Cruz had no choice but to take Jana with them. He and Meg hurried down the hotel hallway, the little girl running to keep pace with them. She chattered, about dinner, about the day, misjudging their anxiety for excitement.

For her, it was just one more adventure.

For Cruz, it was just one more punch in the gut.

When they got to Meg's office, he stepped out in front, blocking their view. One glance told him that that the outer area, Charlotte's domain, was untouched. Sanjoi had his butt perched on the desk. He frowned at Cruz and nodded in Meg's direction.

"It's a real mess in there," he said.

Cruz looked through the connecting door. He could see the backs of two uniformed officers. They were standing in front of the desk. Between their shoulders, he got a glimpse of Detective Myers's face. His eyes were focused down. Cruz took a step forward, the man looked up and Cruz could see a mix of frustration and anger on the detective's face.

He turned to check Jana. Meg had grabbed a stack of yellow legal pads, some red pens and settled the little girl on the leather couch. "Can you please watch her?" she asked Sanjoi.

"Sure. I got one her age at home."

Cruz stepped aside, letting Meg go first. It was her office, after all. But at the last second, he grabbed her hand and hung on. Her fingers were cold.

"Meg. Detective Montoya." Detective Myers greeted them.

It was a repeat of her apartment, sans food. The glass on all the pictures had been broken, books had been shoved off shelves, and the walls and curtains sprayed with paint. Her desk had held up, even though it appeared, based on the dents and nicks in the wood, likely caused by a hammer or a similar tool, that the intruder had tried valiantly to break open the locked drawers.

Everything that had been on the desk was now on the floor. Cruz couldn't focus on that, however. He was too busy looking at the desk. He'd been prepared. After all, they'd been told there was blood. But he hadn't been prepared for the extent. The entire surface of the large desk was covered. A thick mat that had dried, in rough waves and ridges.

The intruder had taken his hand in a circular motion, like he was waxing a car.

"Whose blood is that?" Meg asked, her voice subdued.

Myers shook his head. "Not even sure it's human," he added.

Cruz could feel Meg's grip loosen and he wondered if she was going to faint. "You've seen enough," he said. "Go sit with Jana."

She shook her head. "I left here at shortly after five, just a little over two hours ago. There are cameras in the hallway. He made a mistake. This time we should be able to identify him."

"Your security department has already pulled the tape." Myers walked over to the television and built-in DVD player that hung on Meg's wall. He pressed a button.

The good news was that the camera had been working. The clarity was actually pretty good, certainly better than the grainy image that some cameras captured. The bad news was that the guy had been smart.

He'd worn a jogging suit with the hood up. He'd had a towel draped around his neck and a back-pack slung over one shoulder. Anybody walking past him wouldn't have given him a second look—

would have just assumed that he'd been working out in the hotel gym. He kept his head down the entire time, never giving the camera a look at his face.

The black-and-white tape supported the theory that today's intruder was likely the same person who had pushed Meg toward the canal and then run up the stairs. He was the same height, weight and moved with the same fluid grace.

He opened the outer office door with a key.

When Cruz saw that, he spun around to face Sanjoi who was standing in the doorway. "How would he have gotten a key?"

The man shrugged his thin shoulders. "I don't know. All the executives and their administrative assistants have a key to their own office suite and then there are a few master keys that can unlock any door. But we keep them on a tight string. None of our keys have come up missing lately."

"That doesn't mean they couldn't have been copied."

The man shook his head. "They're all clearly marked as a Do Not Duplicate key."

With the right amount of money, that wouldn't have been too big a problem to get around. And Tom Looney in Maintenance and Troy Blakely in Security would probably have both had access to master keys. He doubted somebody from

Accounts Payable would have had that same access but Mason Hawkins had something better perhaps—the Charlotte connection.

"You have your key?" he asked.

"Yes."

"Okay. We need to ask Charlotte that same question. What's her address?"

"She lives with her mother. She's a lovely lady. I don't want her getting upset."

He cocked his head.

"Oh, fine." She grabbed a sheet of paper off Charlotte's desk and scribbled something down. "Can you not tell her that I know about her and Hawkins? At least until I decide what I should do?"

"I'll do my best." He flipped a button and watched the tape again. When the intruder came out, the camera got a good view of the backpack. Cruz assumed that's where he'd been carrying the blood. It was hard to tell if it looked lighter.

It looked…new. Yes, definitely new.

Cruz studied the intruder. In fact, everything the man had on looked new. His white athletic shoes didn't have a mark on them. The dark jogging suit wasn't faded or stretched out.

Cruz drummed his nails on the desk. It was a long shot but he didn't have much else. "Play that part again," he said.

Detective Myers hit Rewind and when they got to the part where the backpack was visible, Cruz motioned for him to pause the tape. There was a logo on the bag. "I need this frame blown up," he said.

Detective Myers stepped forward. He was stroking his chin, looking thoughtful. "We identify the brand, find out where it's sold locally, and then see if we can trace the purchase."

Cruz nodded, grateful that Myers was tracking with him. But when Meg stepped forward, a puzzled look on her face, he knew she wasn't.

"It's a combination of old-fashioned feet-on-the-street," he explained, "and using available technology. This guy's shoes, jogging suit and backpack all look new. So, maybe he bought them at the same time. If it was recent enough, maybe Detective Myers and his team can jog some store clerk's memories. If that doesn't work, technology may be our friend. Almost everybody captures their sales records electronically now. The store should be able to tell us if they sold shoes, a jogging suit and this brand of backpack in one transaction. There will be a time stamp on the transaction. So, maybe we can get a better photo of him at the store. Or maybe we get even luckier and we can match the transaction code up with credit card activity. Then we have an address."

"You make it sound so easy," Meg said faintly.

Myers shook his head. "Nothing is ever easy. But Cruz is right. We may get lucky, and given that we don't have much else, I'll take luck."

Meg heard a noise. She turned and saw Jana at the door. Before she could react, Cruz had moved. He scooped up the little girl and walked back into the reception area. Meg followed him and saw that Sanjoi was on the phone. He looked up, shrugged and mouthed, "Sorry."

"Hey, don't you have some macaroni and cheese calling your name?" Cruz asked the little girl.

She shook her head. "Macaroni and cheese doesn't talk," she said.

"I know...I meant... Never mind," Cruz said. He tickled the little girl's ribs and she giggled. He glanced back at Meg. "Let's call it a night. Myers and his team will let us know if they find anything." Once they were through the door, he moved close. "Does it make you nervous that in-house security couldn't even contain a four-year-old?"

She smiled, grateful that she still could. He hadn't even needed to tickle her ribs.

Jana poked her head over Cruz's shoulder and looked at Meg. "What happened to your office?" Jana asked.

"It got messed up," Meg said.

"Why?"

Because someone hates me. "I'm not sure, Jana."

"Do you have to clean it up? I always have to clean up my mess. Mommy says."

Cruz turned his head. "I doubt that you'll be able to work in there tomorrow. Myers won't be done with the scene."

Jana twisted in Cruz's arms. "Tomorrow Uncle Cruz and I are going to Six Flags and ride the roller coaster. Can Meg come, too, Uncle Cruz? Please?"

"Meg may have other plans," he said very carefully.

Yes. She definitely should come up with some plans. But right now her head was empty of everything but the absolute horror of seeing her desk covered in dried blood. She wanted to forget it all. "I've never been to Six Flags," she said.

Cruz's eyes lit up. "There's a first time for everything."

Jana seemed to catch the subtle tension that was flowing between the two adults. Her head swiveled from one to the other. "Pretty please," she said, to no one in particular.

Cruz stopped walking, forcing Meg to also stop. "Someone is intent upon creating havoc in my life," she said. "I don't want Jana to be touched by that. The two of you should go."

Cruz considered her protest. "Don't tell anybody

where we're going. Don't tell Slater, Charlotte or anybody else who might be curious. There's no way anybody will know where we'll be."

A whole day without worry over what some crazy person might do next. It sounded like heaven.

"He or she might follow us," Meg said.

Cruz shook his head. "I'll make sure that doesn't happen."

Meg chewed on the corner of her lip. "Okay. I'll go."

CRUZ GOT UP EARLY, checked on both Jana and Meg, who were still sleeping, made sure the bolt lock was secure behind him and left the hotel. Fifteen minutes later, he was waiting at the corner of Charlotte's street, headed toward her house, when she pulled up to the four-way stop. She was alone. He remembered Meg's comment that she didn't want Charlotte's mother to be upset. Maybe the conversation should occur here.

He stepped out of the car and waved her down. She didn't wave back but she didn't take off in her car. He approached the car and she rolled down her window.

"Detective," she said, looking in her rearview mirror.

There was nobody coming. He didn't care. If

someone happened by, they could just go around. "Morning, Charlotte," he said.

"This is a little surprising," she said, irritation evident in her voice.

"Where you headed?" he asked.

She tilted her chin down. "Not that it's any business of yours but I go to a yoga class on Sunday mornings."

He'd never been to a yoga class but something didn't seem right. She was in full makeup and had on a nice shirt and pants. "Yeah, well, I have a couple questions for you," he said. "About your relationship with Mason Hawkins."

Her upper lip twitched. Once, then again. "He worked in accounting. There were times when he'd need to consult with me on an invoice. Look, I don't want to be late."

It was time to cut to the chase. "I saw the two of you yesterday, on the street."

The way her face colored, he suspected that what he'd seen might have been the more platonic part of the day. He let her wonder.

"I don't understand what business it is of yours," she said, obviously deciding the best defense was a whiny offense.

"He's on a short list of people who might have a grudge against Meg. Definitely my business."

She shook her head. "I almost took him off the

list before I gave it to Meg but I couldn't take the chance that she'd remember his departure. He isn't behind any of Meg's problems. He's moved on."

The man was in his boxers in the middle of the afternoon. "Right. How long have the two of you had a thing?"

She shrugged. "We started going out a couple months before he was terminated. So I guess almost a year." She pulled her lip and got lipstick on her front teeth. "Does Meg know about you being here?"

"No," he lied. "She'd be pretty surprised, right?"

"I imagine. He wanted to keep it quiet. He didn't like people knowing his business. He was always asking me if anybody was talking about him."

Hawkins had been using her, maybe trying to keep one step ahead of anybody who was interested in looking at the financials that didn't quite add up. For the first time, Cruz felt almost sorry for her. But he still had an uneasy feeling that there was something off here. He decided to take a chance.

"I suppose Hawkins is an okay guy," he said, "of course, he's no Scott Slater."

She narrowed her eyes. "It wasn't as if I'd have much of a chance there," she said. "Especially considering that *your wife* is ahead of me in line."

Now the claws were coming out. And he felt the

pain of the verbal scratch. Was Meg in line? Were the two women competing for Slater's attention?

If they were, he didn't think Meg realized it. She seemed genuinely fond of Charlotte.

"If I find out that Hawkins had anything to do with any of this, or that you knew about it, I won't hesitate to bring you both down," Cruz said.

"Take your best shot, Detective."

Chapter Twelve

By twenty after seven, Cruz was back at the hotel. Meg and Jana were both dressed and the four-year-old was leaping around the hotel room, as if she was a reindeer on uppers.

"Sorry," he mouthed to Meg.

She smiled. "Where were you?"

He didn't want Charlotte to ruin their day. "I'll tell you later. Let's have breakfast."

They ate in the hotel restaurant. Cruz and Jana both had pancakes and bacon, Meg had oatmeal and fruit. Meg could see a few of the younger, female waitstaff huddled together and thought they were probably speculating on who Cruz was and how Meg came to be eating at his table.

When it came time to leave the hotel, Cruz led them out the back door of the hotel, to a car that was parked in the alley. He reached above the front tire on the driver's side and snagged a key. "Get in," he said.

"What happened to your other rental car?" Meg asked.

"It's still there. I just figured it wouldn't hurt to drive something different."

She didn't know why she was surprised. Cruz always had a plan A, B and C. He'd said that he'd make sure they weren't followed. This was probably just one of many precautions he'd take to keep that promise.

Once he got Jana buckled in, he slid into the driver's seat. He wore green cargo shorts, a white T-shirt and sandals. He looked very much like the man she'd married six years ago.

"Need directions?" she asked.

"I think I've got it," Cruz said.

It was the last thing either of them said to one another. It was not silent, however, in the car. Jana kept up a running monologue. Meg learned about the little girl's favorite colors, her favorite animals, things she would not eat no matter what and why girls were better than boys. When she said, "Girls get to sit to go potty," Cruz smiled. Other than that, he was hard to read.

Or she might have just been perceptively dull. Because her head was whirling. Why had she agreed to this? It was a huge responsibility to bring a four-year-old to an amusement park. There would be big crowds, lots of geography and lots of temptation.

What if she ate something and got sick?

What if she got too much sun?

Oh, God. What if she got lost?

"Maybe we shouldn't go," she said. "You hate crowds."

Cruz turned to look at her. "I'm turning into the parking lot," he said. "We're here."

"But…"

Jana was scrambling out of her car seat. "Let's go," she said.

There was no stopping this train. Maybe she should tie herself to the tracks. It might be less painful. "Okay," she said, opening her door. "Here goes nothing."

There was a line to get in. Jana danced around them. Meg never took her eyes off her. Once they were through the gate, Cruz pulled Jana aside. "Hang on," he said. "We're going to do it all. Every last thing. And eat all kinds of things that have high sugar content. But you need to stay with us and not go running off. And if we get separated, don't leave the park with anyone but Meg or me. No matter what. Come to this spot right here, at the entrance, by the big pink umbrellas. We will find you."

He kept his voice calm but she could tell that

Jana was listening. "I know the rules, Uncle Cruz," she said.

It was a sad world that four-year-olds understood so much.

He smiled. "Good. I hope your aunt Meg does. What's the number one rule, Meg?"

"Have fun?" she asked.

He shook his head. "That's rule number two. Rule number one is, don't sit behind me on the roller coaster if you're going to throw up."

"Hurl," Jana corrected. She bent at the waist and made an exaggerated sound of vomiting. She was smiling when she straightened up. "That's what my mom calls it. Hurling. And when you do it, you have to bend way over." She demonstrated the move again.

Cruz narrowed his eyes. "Your mother could benefit from charm school."

Jana shook her head. "She's *way* too old for school. You try it, Uncle Cruz."

Shaking his head, he bent at the waist and made the obligatory gagging sounds. Jana clapped her hands in approval. "Now you," she said, pointing to Meg.

"Meg doesn't have to—" Cruz said.

"I'll do it." She bent at the waist and gave it her best shot.

"That was pretty good," Jana said. "But you got

to be fast." She whipped the trunk of her small body forward, almost bending double at the waist. Then she did it again, just in case the adults were too dumb to get it the first time.

"Enough," Cruz said. "Let's go."

MEG DIDN'T HURL. Got a little motion-sick once or twice but managed to hold it together. Nothing seemed to bother Jana, except there was one tense moment when it appeared that she might not be tall enough for a ride.

"How tall are you?" Cruz asked, staring at the notice.

She edged up to Cruz, ran a hand across the top of her head and hit him at the waist. "This tall," Jana said.

Cruz looked at Meg. "There you have it," he said.

Fortunately, *this tall* was exactly a half inch more than what she needed. Their next stop was the Ferris wheel and Meg didn't complain when Jana wanted to ride it three times in a row. She loved it just as much. Then it was time for lunch. Meg led the way and they found hot dogs, chips and icy cold slushes. Perfection.

"I want to do the water rides," Jana proclaimed.

Cruz shrugged. "It's a hundred in the shade. Best idea I've heard all day."

Ten minutes later, they were in a small rubber boat, enjoying a perfectly nice gentle water ride, when, out of nowhere, they dropped what had to be fifty feet into a pool of water. Jana squealed and laughed and Meg hoped that her stomach would catch up soon.

She lifted the hem of her soaked blouse.

"Hey," Cruz said, looking around at the crowd.

"It's okay," she said. She pulled off the shirt.

Cruz smiled. "You wore your suit?"

"I knew there were a lot of water rides. And everybody has a cell phone these days," she added.

"And you didn't want to win the wet T-shirt contest," he teased.

She wrinkled her nose and shook her head.

"Always the Girl Scout," he said.

Yeah, well Girl Scouts were supposed to be always prepared and she was totally unprepared three minutes later for the feeling of Cruz's arms around her and Jana as the three of them crowded into another small boat.

It felt so darn good.

And she felt some of the tension in her body ease up.

"Rapids ahead," he warned, his mouth close to her ear. "Hold on."

Maybe he realized her heart was about to flutter right out of her chest.

By late afternoon, Jana was so tired she was starting to trip over her own feet. But she pointed to a sign, advertising that last year's winner of *American Idol* was appearing that night. "I want to go," she said. "I saw her on television."

Cruz shook his head and Jana, who likely wasn't told no very often, started to cry.

"It's okay, sweetie," Meg assured her. "Maybe you can come back again sometime and see her sing. Or maybe see someone else you like. They have all kinds of famous people here. You might get a chance to see someone you like even more."

It wasn't a great explanation but it seemed to calm the child down. "Maybe the Jonas Brothers?" she asked.

"Maybe," Meg said.

Cruz hoisted Jana up onto his shoulders. "Let's go home," he said. He started walking toward the gate.

Once buckled in the car, she was asleep before they got out of the parking lot. "Her legs never stopped moving," Meg said, settling back in her own seat.

"It's amazing," Cruz agreed, checking his mirrors. "How are you doing?"

She was a little sunburned, her swimsuit was still damp from the last water ride, and her fingers were sticky from cotton candy. All in all, she hadn't been better in years. "Good, but I think I need a shower."

"Yeah, me, too. What do you say we eat in tonight?"

"I imagine we can convince Jana to eat some more macaroni and cheese," Meg said.

"If we twist her arm," Cruz agreed. "Seems fair since she's got me pretty much twisted around her little finger."

"Really?" Meg rolled her eyes. "Was it the five rides on that thing that whirled backward that convinced you?"

Cruz shook his head. "I know, I know. Big, tough, Chicago cop is putty in four-year-old's hands. Makes for a great headline."

He'd been a little bit of putty but he'd also held the line when it was important. When the little girl had tried to skip ahead of them, Cruz had pulled her back and gently reminded her that she needed to stay with them. When she'd wanted her second sugar-filled drink of the day, Cruz had gotten her a bottle of water.

He'd be a very good dad someday.

Meg felt her throat close up and she could feel the hot burn of tears building. She turned her head to look out the passenger-side window.

"You okay?" he asked, sounding concerned.

"Oh, sure," she said. "Just want to catch my own nap."

Cruz woke her up a couple blocks from the hotel. They tried to do the same with Jana but she wasn't having any of it. Once Cruz turned over the keys to the valet, he gathered Jana into his arms and carried her into the hotel. When they got to their room, he laid the little girl on the big bed. She never opened her eyes.

"Why don't you shower?" Cruz suggested. "I'll do the same and order room service. What do you want?"

"There's a shrimp pasta that I like," she said, grateful to talk about something mundane like dinner. She walked to her room, undressed and turned the shower on. As she rinsed her body, she reflected upon the day.

She'd done okay.

There'd been a brief moment of panic every time Jana had insisted upon trying something new but she'd managed to control her reactions for the most part. Cruz's calm presence had made all the difference.

He was a rock. Always had been.

Two years into their marriage, when she'd slid off an icy Chicago roadway and hit a telephone pole, almost totaling her car, he'd said nothing about the vehicle. He'd arrived at the scene, checked her over for injuries and held her. A year later when she'd broken her leg in an employee softball game, he'd carried her off the field and teased her that girls didn't know how to slide. Both times he'd been scared. But he'd known that she was even more scared. And he'd never faltered.

She was going to love him forever.

And for his own good, she was going to let him go. Again.

Dinner was already on the table by the time Meg got out of the shower and dressed. Her clothing choices were still limited so she opted for a simple black knit sheath dress, leaving her legs and feet bare.

Jana was still sleeping. "Did you tell her that macaroni and cheese awaits?" Meg asked.

Cruz shook his head. "I think she needs sleep more than food. If she wakes up later and she's hungry, we'll raid the vending machines. It will give my sister another reason to bust my chops when she picks her up tomorrow. And you know how she loves to do that."

The Montoya clan was as close as close could be. It was something Meg had envied. She took a sip of the wine that Cruz had ordered and sighed in appreciation. "I had a good time today," she said.

He put down his fork and studied her. "I guess

it's the kind of thing that I always saw us doing. Before, you know."

Before she'd left him with some lame excuse about needing to find herself. "It's complicated, Cruz. But what happened the other night," she said, deliberately keeping her eyes from straying to the bed, "can't happen again."

He pushed back his chair and stood up. "I don't understand why the hell not? I never stopped loving you, Meg. We can fix whatever is wrong. And…and if things have happened in this last year because we weren't together anymore, I can get past that. I don't want the details because quite frankly, I might want to kill someone. But I'll get past it. I just want you back. Five years from now, I want us to take our son or daughter to the amusement park. I want us to be a family."

He was breaking her heart. He deserved to know the truth. "Cruz, I have—"

His cell phone rang. He glanced at it and frowned. "It's Myers. I better take this."

When she nodded, he punched a button. "Montoya." Then he listened. And all the color drained out of his face. "Thanks for calling," he said finally. "I'll check it out and let you know what I find."

"What?" she asked. Her stomach was cramping up in fear.

"Did you tell anyone that we were going to Six Flags today?" he asked, his tone flat.

She shook her head.

"No one? You're sure?"

"I'm positive. You asked me not to and I didn't. Cruz, you're scaring me. What happened?"

"Did you write it down somewhere? On a desk calendar? Or in your electronic calendar in your computer?"

"No. I didn't know we were going until late last night. I called Charlotte and told her I'd be out of the office today. That's all I said. What is going on?"

"Somebody dropped off a package for Myers at the police station. It was photos. Of the three of us at Six Flags. The bastard was there, taking pictures."

She swallowed hard. "How do we know it was him?"

He took a deep breath before answering. "There was a note. 'She can run but she can't hide.'"

Chapter Thirteen

Meg pushed back her chair, ran to the bathroom and threw up everything she'd eaten. When she was done, her skin felt clammy and her legs were weak. Jana, sweet, innocent Jana, who had laughed her way through the day had been in the sights of a maniac. She'd been in danger. Because of Meg.

It was the continuation of a nightmare that had started so many years ago.

"We must have been followed," she said, as she walked out of the bathroom.

"Are you okay?" he asked.

She waved away his concern. "If you didn't tell anyone and I didn't, either, that's the only reasonable explanation."

"I'm a hundred percent confident that we weren't," he said. He started pacing around the small room, running his hands through his hair.

"Maybe there was a tracking device on our car?"

He shook his head. "No time to set it up. I rented

the car under the name of Milo Martinez and paid for it with a credit card under the same name."

She recognized the name as one he'd used before, when working undercover. If the rental company had checked his driver's license, there would have been one on file in Illinois under that name.

"The car got delivered to the hotel," he continued on. "There was no way for anybody to know it was for us. Even if somebody watched us get into it, they wouldn't have had a chance to tag the car."

She tried to think, to reason, but her brain felt as weak as her legs. "None of it makes sense," she said.

He didn't say anything for a minute. When he did, he surprised her. "Earlier today when we wanted lunch, you knew right where the food was. And you led the way to the water rides, like you knew the park. But you'd said you'd never been there before."

It took her a minute to catch up. "They…uh… have a diagram of the park online. I couldn't sleep last night. I got up sometime around two. I jumped onto the public Wi-Fi here at the hotel."

Cruz stopped pacing.

"Oh, no," Meg said. "Do you think somebody hacked into the public network and looked at what I'd searched for?"

"It's possible. Especially if your site doesn't

have the best encryption. But I think it's more likely your laptop. It's pretty easy to install software on somebody's machine that allows somebody else to see everything they are doing. It could have been installed by somebody who had access to your machine or you may just have opened an email and downloaded something without having a clue."

When would she stop screwing up and putting other people at risk? "I'm sorry, Cruz. I'm just so sorry."

"It's okay," he assured her. "Nothing happened."

"It could have."

He didn't respond. She was right. They'd been less careful today, believing that they were safe. The only way Cruz and Jana would be safe was to be away, far away, from her.

Cruz picked up his phone. "I need to fill Myers in."

She didn't want to hear the conversation. Didn't want to relive it. Instead, she went back to her room and brushed her teeth, hoping to get the horrible taste of despair out of her mouth. When she came back, Cruz had just ended the call. He tossed his phone onto the bed. "Myers is on his way over. He wants to see your laptop and to talk to your computer geeks. He's agreed to let me sit in on the conversation. Can you page the right person and ask them to meet us?"

"Of course." She picked up her phone. Minutes later, she'd arranged for their chief information officer to meet Cruz in the lobby.

Cruz had his hand on the door. "Myers offered to bring a female plainclothes officer with him. She'll be here in the room with you and Jana while I'm gone."

"Is that really necessary?"

"He's getting bolder. I'm not sure what the hell he's going to try next."

THE FEMALE OFFICER was tall, blonde and looked as if she could have stepped out of a *Sports Illustrated* swimsuit edition. Her name was Greta. It made Meg's heart flutter a little when Cruz didn't give the woman any more than a cursory glance.

It had always amazed her that sexy Cruz Montoya had fallen for *her.* It had been so unexpected and so wonderful.

She'd had so little experience, having dated a few times before Missy's death but not after. She'd studied, worked and tried to ignore the whispers behind her back. When her dad had lost his job, everyone knew it was because she'd done a terrible thing.

It stopped feeling safe in Maiter, especially after

rocks got thrown through their living room window and their house almost burned down after someone started a fire in their overgrown backyard.

They left Maiter in the middle of the night, like criminals. Her parents found a small house in Houston and she hoped that life would return to normal. But it had taken months for her dad to find work. Every day she saw her mother get angrier and her father more depressed.

She wasn't surprised when the two of them decided to quit pretending that it was okay. The divorce happened quickly. Her dad moved to Austin and she stayed in the house with her mother. When her opportunity to go to college came, she took the first bus out of town.

Chicago had been her fresh start. She was no longer Margaret Mae. She was Meg. And every bit as carefree and cool as any other eighteen-year-old girl. On the outside. She worked hard to hide that there were many nights she didn't sleep. She would wake up to the soft snores of her roommate sleeping close in the crowded dorm room. She'd pull her quilt up to her neck. It couldn't stop the shaking. Or the terror of reliving the night a two-year-old turned blue and died.

Her mother had gotten sick when she was a sophomore and had been dead by the middle of her senior year. Pancreatic cancer was a cruel beast. Her dad had come to the funeral and had wanted her to come live with him after graduation. She'd have done it but then, exactly thirty-three days later, he'd been killed when a semi crossed the middle line.

And she was truly alone.

She stayed in Chicago after graduation and was happy when The Montray, a wonderful hotel in the high-rent shopping district, offered her an internship.

She worked hard and the internship turned into a full-time job. The people in the big hotel became her family. She loved the complexity of the place, everything from making sure the huge flower arrangements for the lobby got delivered to ensuring that visiting royalty was happy with the thread count in their sheets. She worked in registration, at the front counter, in group sales, in marketing, in accounting and even suffered through a brief stint in the massive kitchen, where she mostly tried to stay out of the way.

She got promoted a couple times and was already a manager when she met Cruz. His mother had introduced them. When they were dating, she'd tell him stories of the crazy things that happened at work. He'd roll his eyes and say pithy things about people who had more money than common sense. During their marriage, she got promoted to director. Cruz had been proud of her. And she'd known that he bragged about her at work. After Cruz and Sam Vernelli became partners, Sam would tease her, tell her that he hoped she never fell off her pedestal.

She'd tried. But pedestals were not always steady and when Cruz started talking about babies, the ground started to shake. She'd been quiet at first, then tried to gently remind him of all the reasons that things were perfect just the way they were. But when he'd started talking about parochial schools, club soccer and advanced calculus, all the things their children would have and do, the shaking advanced to full-blown quaking and the pedestal became very unstable.

Missy had never done any of those things.

Because of her.

She couldn't tell Cruz the truth. Didn't want him to realize that he'd been a fool to put her on the pedestal. Instead, she'd let him think that the pedestal had bored her, that it either wasn't high enough, low enough or some combination thereof. Left him confused, angry, and unable to sort through the mess.

And now she'd led him straight into another bit of craziness. He should run like hell because the pedestal was about to topple over and crush him.

She glanced away from the television that she was watching but not seeing. She got up and peeked in at Jana, who had gotten up shortly after Cruz had talked to Detective Myers, eaten a few bites of her macaroni, and then fallen asleep again in Meg's bed just minutes after Greta had arrived. She was still sleeping soundly, her pretty little face all relaxed and peaceful.

Peace. Meg could hardly remember the feeling.

She partially closed the connecting door and turned to Greta, who was watching her. "Would you like some coffee or anything?"

The woman shook her head. "No, thank you. Harry and I just finished dinner when your husband, I mean ex-husband, called."

It took Meg a moment to realize that *Harry* was Harold Myers. "You and Detective Myers?" she asked, before she could censor herself.

The woman's face turned pink. "We've been living together for a year. There's no reporting relationship between the two of us but we still try to be discreet."

It seemed an unlikely pairing but then again, what room did she have to talk? Cruz had come from a sometimes loud, highly charged family. They talked rough, they hugged hard and they counted on each other. Her family had been quiet and emotionless, even in the wake of Missy's death. They didn't talk about what happened. The one time she had been brave enough to broach the subject, her father had told her that she should have been more careful and her mother had said that it was best to try to forget it.

She stopped trying to talk about it and stopped hoping to count on anyone else. She sure as heck didn't want anyone counting on her.

She kept a safe zone around her and the only one that had ever breached it was Cruz. In his bold, in-your-face way, he'd managed to get past all the imaginary alligators and scale the palace walls.

They'd been a team. A cohesive unit.

They'd loved and laughed and in the quiet nights when she awoke and she could hear Cruz breathing next to her, she'd been overwhelmed at the love she felt for him.

Yet she'd continued to keep her secret.

Maybe because she really liked the pedestal. Maybe because she was afraid of disappointing him. Maybe because she'd gotten used to never talking about it and now it just seemed too damn late.

She heard two sharp raps on the door. "Meg, it's Cruz."

Greta opened the door. He came in with Detective Myers on his heels. They didn't have her laptop.

"Well?" she asked, impatient to have the details.

Cruz gave her a tired smile. "There was a program on your laptop. Basically, it was recording and transmitting every keystroke, every website you went to, all the activity."

She felt nauseous and terribly violated. "Transmitting it where?"

"We're working on that," Myers said. "Every computer has an address, sort of like a house number. But whoever installed this was smart. When our technical guys try to trace the address, it's bouncing them all over the place. Russia. China. India. The guy was good at covering his tracks. Unfortunately, it's likely that we're not going to have much success."

"Why?" she demanded. This was getting old. She wanted answers.

"Two things. First of all, the malware was pretty sophisticated. The technical guys knew what they were looking for and they had trouble finding it on the machine. Two, he has to assume that once he sent the pictures, we'd eventually find our way to your laptop. By now, he's probably covering his cyber-tracks. Your information is probably being routed through some old lady's desktop in Indonesia and she's as innocent of the crime as you are."

Meg shook her head. "I hate computers."

Cruz nodded. "Me, too."

She mostly used her laptop for personal reasons. Online shopping, reading the *Wall Street Journal,* perusing new recipes. What had someone hoped to gain by tracking that kind of activity? "How did this program get on my computer?"

Cruz ran a hand through his long hair. His face was very serious. "That much we know. You didn't open some random email and install this. Somebody who had access to your laptop downloaded the software."

She didn't know if that was supposed to make her feel better or worse that she hadn't been fooled by some slick cyber-creep. "How long?" she asked. "How long has this been going on?"

"For almost six months," Myers said.

She mentally reviewed the termination dates of Hawkins, Looney and Blakely. Six months ago they'd all still been working at the hotel. Oscar Warren had also been there. She looked at Cruz's face and knew that he'd already gone through the same exercise.

"Where do you normally keep your laptop?" Detective Myers asked.

She shrugged. "At home, usually. I bring it to work occasionally."

"When it's at work, do you have it with you? Do you take it to meetings?"

"No. I leave it in my office. I'll use it during my lunch hour. Sometimes I'll stop at a coffee shop on my way home and jump on the public Wi-Fi. I don't see how this could have happened, I have a password on it."

"There are programs that can break a password in seconds. Child's play for somebody who knows what they're doing."

"Charlotte would have had access," Cruz said. "Because of his relationship with her, Hawkins probably did, too. You said that you'd come back to the office and he'd be hanging around."

She nodded.

"And Looney was in Maintenance and Blakely in Security. Both with access to a master key that could have been used to unlock the office when both you and Charlotte were away."

Her head was spinning. "Yes."

"Oscar Warren?" he asked.

She shook her head. "We didn't give keys to any of the people from A Hand Up."

"Slater would have had a key," Cruz stated.

"What?" Meg asked.

"I've been focusing my attention on these four white men. One because of his jail record and three because their employment was terminated within the last year. But maybe it's a white guy with a whole other agenda. I don't want to be stupid and overlook somebody."

Cruz had never been stupid. "It's not Scott," she said.

"Nobody gets a free pass, Meg. Nobody."

She needed the free pass. "I'm going to bed," she said. "It was nice to meet you," she said, looking at Greta. "Thank you for coming to stay with me."

"Do you want me to get Jana?" Cruz asked.

Meg didn't want to disturb the little girl. She shook her head. "She can sleep with me."

Five minutes later, she heard the doors and knew that Detective Myers and Greta had left. Seconds later, Cruz was standing at her door. "Sleeping?" he asked quietly.

She could pretend. "No," she said.

He crossed the room and sat on the edge of the bed. The lights were all off, with the exception of one dim light from the bathroom. His shape was visible but she couldn't see the expression on his face. She could feel warmth roll off his big body.

"Are you okay?" he asked.

"I think so," she lied. "I'm sorry about this, Cruz. Sorry that you got dragged into it and that it touched Jana. I never meant for that to happen."

"It's not your fault, Meg."

She didn't answer. Couldn't. What if it really was her fault? What if it had something to do with what had happened to Missy?

They sat there in the dark for a long moment. Finally, Cruz shifted. "Is there anything you haven't told me, Meg?" he asked, his voice soft.

She swallowed hard. "Of course not," she said. "Why?"

"I don't know," he said. "But just a few minutes ago, right before Myers and Greta left, you had the strangest look on your face. Like you were thinking of something."

"I don't know what you're talking about," she said. "Look, Cruz, I'm really tired." She rolled over, giving him her back.

And she didn't start to cry until he'd left the room.

Chapter Fourteen

Early Monday morning, Cruz got Jana dressed and fed her breakfast in the hotel restaurant. She was barely finished with her pancakes when Elsa came to pick her up. It was a tearful reunion, on Elsa's part. Jana was all smiles and gave Cruz a big kiss. He watched them drive away and then did something that he'd never expected to do—not in a hundred years. He initiated a background check on Meg.

He dialed and Sam answered on the fourth ring. "Vernelli," he said, his voice rough.

"It's almost eight o'clock your time, partner," Cruz said. "Get your sorry self out of bed."

Sam sighed. "Claire and I took the red-eye back from Omaha. She wanted to spring the news about the baby to her parents in person."

Cruz had only met the Fontaines once, at Sam and Claire's wedding. They'd been nice enough but rather reserved. "How'd that go?"

"Better than either of us might have expected."

That was no doubt a good thing because if the Fontaines had given Claire even a moment of grief, Sam would have told them to stuff it and he'd have whisked his new bride away from Nebraska and back to Chicago. "How's Claire feeling?"

"As long as I embrace my role of saltine cracker-bearing slave, it's all good," Sam said. "What's going on with you? How's Meg?" he asked, his tone careful.

Cruz understood the caution. Sam had lived through the death spiral that Cruz had started when Meg had suddenly announced she was leaving. "Meg's okay. I mean, she looks great, she's doing really well in her job, she…" Cruz couldn't finish. He sucked in a breath. This was his best friend. "She's in trouble, Sam. And I'm not sure she's telling me the truth."

There was silence on the other end.

Cruz barged on. "I need your help. I want to know everything about Margaret Mae Gunderson Montoya that there is to know. I'm not sure what's important and what's not, so don't leave anything out."

"Consider it done. I'll be in touch."

Cruz disconnected the call. When he'd talked to Myers the night before, the man had told him that the blood on Meg's desk had been analyzed. The good news was that it wasn't human. It was canine. But not from just one dog. Three dogs. The bastard had killed three dogs. They figured he'd somehow managed to collect the blood and then he'd smeared it across Meg's desk.

They were dealing with somebody who had a screw loose. Technologically sharp, yet bent. It was a scary combination. He hoped the guy didn't build bombs in his basement.

Cruz punched an address into his GPS that he'd gotten from Tom Looney's employment application. The man had worked at a factory before he'd been hired on at the hotel. He'd listed his supervisor as H. Looney. It wasn't that common of a last name and Cruz was betting on the fact that H. Looney was some kind of relation.

Who hopefully knew just where Tom Looney could be found.

When he arrived at the small shop and asked for H. Looney, the woman at the front desk pushed a button and the overhead page went out. "Haney to the front. Haney to the front."

In less than a minute, a fifty-year-old man who was wiping his hands on a grease rag poked his head around the door. "What can I do for you?" he asked.

"I'm Detective Cruz Montoya. I'm looking for Tom Looney. I know he used to work here."

The man nodded. "He's my nephew. He worked

here for a couple years after he lost his job at the prison."

There hadn't been anything on his application about working at a prison. "What did he do at the prison?"

"Maintenance supervisor. I guess it was budget cuts. He'd worked there a couple years."

Maybe. Or maybe he'd screwed up there, too, and didn't want anybody checking those references. "I stopped by his house yesterday. The woman living there didn't seem to know where he was."

The man smiled. "Donnetta. Now that's a hard nut to crack. She's Bertie's sister. Tom's mother," he added. "I'm his uncle on his daddy's side."

"Where's your nephew now?"

"Doing maintenance work at the food plant south of town, on I-37. It's a good job." Haney Looney reached into the pocket of his overalls and pulled out a worn billfold. He opened it and thumbed through a stack of business cards, pulling one out from near the bottom. "Here. He gave this to me just a couple weeks ago."

Cruz took the card. "Okay. Here's the deal. I'm going to pay your nephew a visit. I don't really expect you to keep this conversation to yourself. I understand how family works. But understand this. If he suddenly goes AWOL, I'm not going to reflect positively upon that."

"I'm not going to call him. He's a man. Or at least he says he is. He can answer his own damn questions." The man turned and left the room.

It took Cruz thirty minutes to get to the food plant and another fifteen to work his way past the guards at the various entrances. The place was tied up tighter than Fort Knox. A sign of the times for sure. No manufacturer in their right mind wanted to make it easy for someone to get inside, tamper with some product and make a couple hundred people sick before the company could get the product off the shelves.

He asked the receptionist to get a manager. She pushed a button, spoke into her headset and in just minutes he was invited into the offices.

The manager was a woman, probably close to fifty. She wore blue pants, a blue shirt and a white lab coat. Cruz gave her his card, explained that he was investigating a crime and that he needed to talk to Tom Looney. She didn't ask any questions, just led him to a conference room.

It took Tom Looney ten minutes to get to the room. He was wearing a hairnet over his ponytail and there was a pair of safety glasses in his pocket. He was also sweating.

Cruz didn't waste any time. He slid another card

across the table. "I'm here to talk to you about some trouble that Meg Montoya has been having."

Looney didn't say anything.

"We can do this the easy way or the hard way," Cruz said. "I don't much care. But I'm thinking your employer might not like the idea of you needing time off unexpectedly to give a statement to the police."

Looney shook his head in apparent disgust. "I don't know what some crazy guy attacking her at the fundraiser has to do with me."

Now that was interesting. To the best of Cruz's knowledge, the incident hadn't made the papers. "How do you know about that?"

The man's face got red. He hesitated, chewing on his top lip. "I know someone who was there."

"Define *someone*."

The man pursed his lips. Finally, he spoke. "The hotel employed four men from the prison through the A Hand Up program. I live with one of the men. He told me about it."

The pieces were starting to click together. The uncle's strange comment—*"He's a man or at least he says he is."* The missing work experience on the job application. Cruz leaned forward. "You used to work at the prison. But you got fired from there for having a personal relationship with one of the inmates, didn't you?"

The man nodded. "Look. I don't want any trouble at this job. I work with a bunch of rednecks. It's bad enough to be a gay man but to be a gay man living with an ex-con is just asking for trouble."

No doubt about that.

"You lost your job at the hotel, too," Cruz said.

"That was for a totally different reason. I missed too much work."

"Why?"

"My partner was ill. He needed surgery and couldn't drive for several weeks. He had therapy appointments afterward and there was nobody else to take him. I ran out of vacation time."

Cruz knew that if Looney had told Meg the truth, there was a high likelihood that he'd have kept his job. But he understood the secrecy. This *was* Texas, after all.

"Meg has had some other things happen. Do you have any idea of who might want to antagonize her or hurt her in some way?" Cruz asked.

The man shook his head. "She's a good person. Probably the nicest manager I've ever worked with. I was the one who told her about the A Hand Up program. She knew I had some personal connection but she never pried. I can't see anybody wanting to hurt her. I guess the only advice I could give you is to talk to her secretary. That woman's a bitch."

CRUZ TURNED HIS attention to finding Troy Blakely. The guy had worked at the jewelry store for over a year. He had to have had lunch in the area, or maybe dropped off some dry cleaning. The possibilities were endless. People left tracks everywhere.

He hit pay dirt at his fourth stop—a small Thai restaurant. The waitress, a tired-looking thirtysomething blonde, looked at the picture and smiled. "He used to stop in a couple nights a week. Always had a beer while he was waiting for his food. Nice enough guy, although there was something about him that gave me the creeps."

"When's the last time you saw him?"

"A week or so ago."

That surprised Cruz. There were a lot of places to get Thai food. If he wasn't working in the area, was he living nearby?

"Anything unusual?"

"I asked him if he'd found work. A few months back he'd lost his job at this big hotel."

"Had he?"

"I'm not sure. I remember his answer because it was sort of weird. He said it didn't matter because he was finally going to be able to fix everything."

Fix everything.

It could mean a thousand things. "He ever have

a conversation with anybody else while he was waiting for his beer?"

She shook her head. "No. I suppose I was the only one who paid much attention to him. To be honest, I felt a little sorry for him. When he first started coming in, which was probably a good year ago, he'd said that his parents had died recently—the way he talked about them, I got the impression that they were really close."

"His parents live in San Antonio?"

A door slammed near the rear of the restaurant and she started wiping the counter in earnest. "I need to go help put away stock," she said.

"His parents?" he prompted again.

She wrinkled her brow. "Some small town two hours away. Hollyville. Haileyville. Something like that."

Cruz discreetly passed her a fifty-dollar bill and a card with his name and number. "Thank you. If you remember anything else, please call me."

It took Cruz five minutes to locate Haileyville, Texas, on the map. He didn't bother to plug the address into his GPS. It was a hundred miles west, then a short twenty miles north—main highways all the way.

He grabbed coffee and two candy bars from the gas station and settled in for the trip. He was barely at the outskirts of San Antonio when he called Meg.

"Meg Montoya," she answered

"How's your day?"

"I had a couple meetings and quite a bit of voice mail and email to get through."

His idea of hell. He hated the bureaucratic nature of police work that required writing reports and documenting endless conversations. Hated going to meetings where decisions never got made. Hated listening to consultants who couldn't find their butts unless someone put a dollar sign on them.

"Lucky you," he said. "Hey, I'm headed out of town. I got a lead on Troy Blakely. His parents lived in Haileyville. It's about two hours west of here."

Meg knew exactly where Haileyville was. It was thirty miles from her hometown of Maiter, Texas. They'd gone school shopping there and Christmas shopping, too. It was significantly bigger than Maiter, although that wasn't saying much. Probably had ten thousand residents. Maiter had boasted they'd hit a thousand when the Wyman triplets had been born.

Cruz's trip shouldn't make her nervous but it did. Nobody in Haileyville was going to be talking about something that happened twenty years ago, some thirty miles away.

"Will you be back tonight?" Meg asked.

"Yes. I'd really appreciate it if you would either be in your office or in our rooms. Please don't leave the hotel."

"I won't," she said. She didn't need to leave the hotel in order to do what needed to be done.

"Thank you," he said.

She disconnected before she did something stupid like beg him to be careful. Then she pulled out Detective Myers's card from her purse and dialed his office number.

"Myers," he answered.

She could just see his stubby, nicotine-stained fingers grabbing his desk phone.

"This is Meg Montoya. I need to tell you something."

Chapter Fifteen

When Cruz got to Haileyville, he searched for funeral homes on his smart phone. There were four. The first one he tried was closed but the second one had lights on. He rang the bell. A man in his mid-forties, wearing a black suit and shiny black shoes, opened the door.

"May I help you?" the man asked, his tone hopeful. Cruz understood. In a town this size, the four funeral homes would be in fierce competition. "My name is Detective Cruz Montoya. I'm investigating a case and I'm trying to find information on this man." He flashed Blakely's picture. "It's my understanding that his parents died, maybe about a year ago. Do you recognize him?"

The man studied the picture, then shook his head. "Perhaps one of his siblings handled the arrangements. What's the name?"

"Troy Blakely."

The man tapped his chin and Cruz saw that his nails were very clean. Probably bad for business to have embalming fluid under the thumbnail. "Now I've got it. You've got the timing right. It was almost a year ago. If you'll follow me, we can look it up." The man led him to a back room, done in tasteful gray and maroon. The man motioned for Cruz to sit and took his own seat in front of an old desktop computer. After a few clicks of the mouse, he stopped. "Here we are. Blakely. Gloria and Ted. Sad situation really. The woman died and the husband arranged the funeral. At the same time, he prepaid for his own services. That's not all that strange. However, we realized he had something in mind when just three days later, we were advised that he was also deceased. A deliberate overdose on his wife's medication."

"Their family?"

"No family. I assisted in the writing of his wife's death notice for the local paper and specifically asked him about children. He did mention that his wife had lost a daughter from a previous marriage many years ago but he didn't want us to mention that in the newspaper."

"No son? You're sure?"

"As sure as I can be. No mention of one and he definitely wasn't at either funeral."

Cruz wanted to pound his head on the table. It wasn't making sense. It had to be the right couple. Same last name. The waitress had the name of the town right.

But no son. Troy Blakely had made it sound like he was very close to his parents.

Something did not smell right.

"What's their address?"

The funeral director frowned. "I'm not sure I should release that."

Cruz cocked an eyebrow. "Who's going to complain? They're dead and there's no family."

The man nodded. "I suppose you're right. And we, of course, want to cooperate with the police." He wrote something on a slip of paper and passed it across the desk to Cruz. "Good luck, Detective."

Cruz plugged the address into his GPS and found the small house in less than ten minutes. It was a modest ranch on a quiet street, with concrete birds and rabbits and even a few frogs in the flower garden.

Had they belonged to the Blakelys? Were they left behind in the garage, no longer a concern for a man determined to follow his wife?

He knocked and a minute later, a young woman opened the door. She had a baby, dressed in pink and white, perched on a hip. "Yes," she said, her tone guarded.

"Hi," he said, trying for relaxed. It was a struggle when he was strung tight. "I thought Gloria and Ted Blakely lived here." It was as good an opening line as any. It was possible the new owner had learned something about the previous owners from helpful neighbors.

She shook her head and swayed in the way that all young mothers seemed to know. His sister and sister-in-laws had come home from the hospital knowing how. He stared at the baby. Cute kid. Not much hair. He was about to lift his gaze when the baby flashed him a gummy grin that lit up her face.

At that moment, he'd never envied his partner more. In a few short months, Sam would come home to pure sweetness. Sure, there'd be dirty diapers and sleepless nights but it wouldn't matter. Because there'd be love. Unconditional love.

"They've been gone for almost a year," the woman said, bringing Cruz back. "They both died. We got the house for a good price. Guess it freaked some people out that the man had killed himself here."

"Any family?" he asked.

The woman shook her head. "I guess not."

This was going nowhere fast. "Thanks for your time," he said, giving the baby one last look. He turned, walked down the sidewalk to the house next door, and knocked on the red door. A woman with a square body and a round face answered. Cruz guessed her age to be about sixty.

"My name is Cruz Montoya," he said, holding his card steady so that she could read the information. "I was hoping to talk to someone who knew Gloria or Ted Blakely."

She shrugged and her housedress lifted on one side. "I suppose I knew them as well as anybody. They kept to themselves a lot."

"What about family?"

"Poor things. They didn't have anybody. Not like me and Bert with our five." She leaned forward so far that Cruz thought she might topple over. "I think they might have lost a child," she said, her voice a mere whisper. "One time when I was visiting, I had to use their bathroom." She patted her abdomen. "Five babies and your bladder ain't what it used to be."

Maybe he should tell his sister. She kept complaining that her breasts were sagging. It would give her a whole new body part to worry about.

"I happened to see in their bedroom. There was a pink cross hanging next to the dresser. "It had a name on it. I think it was Missy."

Cruz pulled out the picture of Troy Blakely. "Did you ever see a man who looked like this hanging around?"

She shook her head. "I don't think so. But then again, I don't see so good anymore."

"Is there anybody else who might have known them?" he asked.

She pointed at the house across the street. "You could talk to the Moulins. Of course, neither Debi nor Frank gets home from work until after five."

He wouldn't make it back to San Antonio until after seven-thirty. He didn't want to leave Meg alone for that long. "Thanks for your help," he said. He got in his car and headed east.

DETECTIVE MYERS LISTENED to Meg's story without interruption or expression. He sat in a visitor chair, she sat behind her desk. When she finished, she realized she was clenching her hands together. "Well?" she prompted. She'd spewed her guts. He could at least answer.

"I appreciate you telling me," he said. "I'd have liked to have known right away but that's a moot point now. I take it your ex-husband doesn't know any of this."

She nodded. "I'd like to keep it that way."

"I don't have any compelling reason to tell him," he said. "But he's a smart guy and from what I can tell, a good cop. If he starts digging, he might stumble upon it."

That's what she was afraid of.

"You don't have any reason to believe what's happening now has anything to do with what happened twenty years ago?" Myers asked.

"No. But something unusual did happen today, shortly after I called you. I don't want to make too big a deal out of it but I want you to know about it."

"What was that?"

"I had a visitor. Or so Tim Burtiss said. I had to run upstairs to Scott's office and when I got back he told me that some old lady had come by. He said she seemed sort of nervous and that she asked to see Margaret Mae."

"Margaret Mae?"

"That's what everyone called me when I was a kid."

Detective Myers nodded. "When you lived in Maiter?"

"Yes. And before that, when I lived in Houston. I didn't go by Meg until college."

"What did Tim tell her?"

"He told her the office was Meg Montoya's and she said that's who she wanted. Tim said that he asked the woman for her name, to check it against the list and that she got real pale. He thought she might fall over. She never did give him her name. Just walked away."

"And you have no idea who she was?"

"No. I asked Tim what she looked like and he said that she wasn't much over five feet. Kind of round. Pretty old, too. Maybe sixty."

Detective Myers smiled. "Tim evidently hasn't heard that sixty is the new forty." He closed his notebook. "But you don't know that this person had anything to do with what happened twenty years ago in Maiter. Maybe it was somebody who lived across the street from you when you were five and you lived in Houston?"

Maybe. But she had a horrible feeling that it had something to do with a secret that she'd managed to hide for half her lifetime.

She needed Cruz to go back to Chicago before all her lies started to unravel. Getting him to agree was going to be difficult, almost impossible.

There was probably only one way. It went against everything she believed in but she was desperate.

"You might be right," she said. She stood up and he did the same. She walked around her desk, across her office, and opened the door. Charlotte was at her desk, her hands on her computer keyboard. The woman looked up but didn't say anything.

Meg shook the detective's hand. "Thank you for coming so quickly."

Detective Myers nodded and left.

Charlotte was staring at her. Meg just shook her head. "No calls for a little while, please," she said. She went into her office, shutting the door behind her. Then she picked up the telephone and put her plan in motion.

WHEN CRUZ GOT BACK to the hotel, he went to Meg's hotel room and was disappointed when it was empty. She had always worked hard and it didn't look as if she changed her pattern. He took the elevator down to the first floor.

There was no security guard outside her office. He started running. When he grabbed the door handle and realized the office was locked, he felt marginally better. Meg had probably ended her day and sent the security guard on his way.

But where the hell was she? She'd promised that she wouldn't leave the hotel. He pulled out his cell phone and punched up her number. It rang three times before she answered it.

"Hello," she said.

"Are you okay?" he asked.

"I...uh...yes, I'm fine," she said. "Just a little busy."

She sounded as if she was out of breath. Maybe she'd gone to the hotel gym. "Where are you?"

"With Scott," she said.

Cruz's chest got tight when his mind immediately conjured up the kind of exercise that the two of them could be getting. *Get a grip, Montoya.* "Working late?" he forced himself to ask.

"Not so much," she said. "Look, Cruz. Scott and I have been talking."

Okay. Talking wasn't bad.

"And I...I am moving into his suite."

Worse than bad. Going over a cliff bad. The first time she'd left, he'd been left to wonder. Now she was painting a real clear picture. He was speechless.

"Cruz?" she prompted.

"You couldn't tell me this in person?" he asked.

"Uh...no. But Scott said he'd like to talk to you."

He wanted to break the man's neck, not talk to him. But before he could hang up, Slater was on the line.

"Cruz, it's not that Meg and I aren't grateful for your help. But we've got this covered. We really think it would better for all of us if you went back to Chicago tonight."

Cruz's legs felt weak. He leaned back against the wall and sank until he was sitting on the floor. He didn't even care if he was on some security camera. What did it matter if he looked pathetic? He was.

He hung up. He had nothing to say to Slater.

Damn them both. He sat on the cool tile floor, feeling nothing. He was numb. He had been so stupid, had actually believed that Meg coming to his bed meant something.

And now she was jumping into Slater's bed.

It made getting shot seem like a walk in the park.

Better for all of us if you went back to Chicago tonight. Well, he sure as hell wasn't going to stick around and watch, or congratulate the happy couple when they finally made their way down to breakfast.

He got up and walked down the hallway. He opted for the stairs instead of the elevator, wanting to physically exert himself. Better that than stick a fist through a wall.

It took him less than five minutes to pack up. Like some sick fool, he checked her closet. She hadn't moved her things yet. He ran his hand across the peach suit that she'd worn that first day. She'd looked so pretty, so professional.

He closed the door of her closet and left the suite. He didn't bother to check out—Slater could handle that—he was handling everything else. He waited for the valet to get his rental car, sure that they were wondering why he'd had them park it less than fifteen minutes ago if he planned on leaving again so soon.

Nothing much was going how he'd planned.

Once the valet delivered his car, he got in, cranked up the air and turned toward the airport. His phone rang and he saw that it was Sam.

"Montoya," he answered, hoping like hell that he didn't start to wail in front of his friend.

"I got the scoop on Meg," Sam said.

The only scoop that mattered was that Meg had chosen Slater. But Cruz kept his mouth shut. He wasn't ready to talk about it yet. "Okay," he said.

"Born in Houston. Parents were married. No other siblings. Lived there until she was fourteen. Then the family moved to Maiter, Texas, where they lived for a couple years. Family moved back to Houston. Parents got divorced about a year afterward. Meg lived with her mother until she went away to college in Chicago. Neither parent remarried, both are now deceased. Meg stayed in Chicago after college. You know the rest."

Meg had told him that she'd grown up in Houston. She'd never mentioned Maiter. Had said that her parents were divorced and both deceased.

"I appreciate you getting back to me," Cruz said. "I'll see you tomorrow. I'm on my way back to Chicago."

There was a long silence on the line. "Are you okay?" Sam asked finally.

"Dandy," Cruz said. "Just dandy." He hung up. Then he called Detective Myers.

The man answered on the second ring. "I was just about to call you," he said. "We've made contact with all the major retail stores in town to ask them to review their transactions to see if anyone purchased shoes, a jogging suit and a backpack recently. I've already heard back from a couple but no luck. The rest said they could get back to me within forty-eight hours."

"That's good," Cruz said. Myers was competent. Cruz wasn't needed here. Did he need it written across the damn sky? "I…uh…wanted to touch base with you. I'm leaving today."

"That surprises me."

"Yeah, well, it's time," Cruz said. There was no need to go into the details. He'd been dumped. Again.

"Does Meg know?" Myers asked.

"She does. Look, I wanted you to know what I found today. There's a waitress who worked at a restaurant that Troy Blakely frequented here in San Antonio. She knows him. Said that he mentioned that he was from Haileyville. Do you know where that is?"

"Yes."

"I drove there today. His parents both died about a year ago, the woman from natural causes, the husband three days later from suicide. What's odd is that Troy wasn't mentioned in the obituary and the neighbors I spoke with weren't familiar with a son."

"Then how do you know you had the right family?"

"The details that he gave the waitress match the details of the deaths. There's something here, I'm just not sure what it is."

There was a pause on the other end of the line. Finally, Myers spoke. "But you're not going to keep looking?"

Now it was Cruz's turn to weigh his words. "I can't. Meg made it pretty clear that she doesn't need my help."

Chapter Sixteen

Meg had felt lousy for days. She was tired and she knew she wasn't eating well—nothing sounded good, not even the pasta that she normally enjoyed. She attributed her general malaise to guilt over how she'd treated Cruz. She'd hurt him again.

He deserved so much better. She'd known that a year ago, when she'd left him the first time. Had remembered it six months ago when she'd stood over his bedside, watching him battle back from a bullet. That time she'd been able to walk away before she did any more damage.

But she hadn't been nearly as strong this time. She'd made a colossal mistake in sleeping with him. She'd given him reason to think that there was a possibility of a reunion.

Now he must really hate her.

She hadn't heard from him since he'd left three weeks ago. Had desperately wanted to talk to him to make sure he was okay. Had even reached for the phone a couple times but had stopped herself. What would she say?

I lied. Again. And this time it's even worse. I asked Scott to lie, too.

She'd gone to Scott's office that afternoon after Cruz had called her on his way back from Haileyville, knowing that she needed to do something very quickly to get Cruz to drop his investigation.

She'd told Scott half the truth. Had admitted that there were unresolved issues between her and Cruz and had asked for his help in convincing Cruz that the two of them were involved. Scott had had only one question. *Does this mean it's over between the two of you? For good?*

She'd said yes. And later, when she heard his side of the conversation with Cruz, was grateful that he played it just right. When he'd asked her to dinner the next night, she'd said yes again. And twice more since then. They'd been very discreet, of course, always leaving the River Walk area and Meg had taken a cab back to the hotel, not wanting the valets to see Scott dropping her off.

Still, she was acutely conscious that their relationship had changed. In meetings, she was hypersensitive to how she responded to his questions or comments. There'd been one really awkward moment in the elevator. They'd been alone and discussing evening plans and Charlotte had gotten in.

Meg had gotten flustered and when she'd gotten back to her office, had realized that her neck had pink blotches on it.

She had hoped that Charlotte hadn't seen it but the woman had been treating her coldly for days now so she thought that wasn't likely.

Charlotte's imagination was no doubt conjuring up images that were significantly more risqué than reality. Each of the dinners had ended with a brief kiss. Neither kiss had been as awkward as their first kiss three months earlier but neither had felt right, either.

Meg knew that Scott was deliberately taking things slow. She appreciated his consideration but thought that a hundred years might not be enough time for her to forget the shape of Cruz's mouth, the taste of him, the heat.

It wasn't fair to Scott. And she intended to tell him that tonight at dinner. But she hadn't counted on a flu bug weighing her down.

She picked up her phone, dialed her doctor's office, waited five minutes on hold and let out a sigh of relief when the receptionist told her that there was a cancellation and the doctor could see her if she could get there in thirty minutes.

Meg shut down her laptop, straightened the papers on her desk and walked out of her office. Charlotte was at her desk, labeling file folders.

"I have an appointment off-site. I should be back within an hour or so," Meg said. "Do you want me to pick you up a sandwich on my way back?"

Charlotte shook her head. "Mother needs a bone density test. I was going to ask to take an early lunch."

"That's fine. Take whatever time you need. I'll catch up with you later."

Meg's doctor's office was ten blocks from the hotel. Normally, she walked it. But today, she had the valet hail her a cab. She didn't feel up to the walk and she didn't want to tempt fate.

For the past three weeks, since Cruz had left, nothing had happened. No more notes, calls or vandalism. It was the one good thing. It made her think that maybe Cruz's questions had spooked somebody. Was it possible that the person responsible for all the havoc had decided that the police were getting too close?

Whatever the reason, Meg was grateful. Just yesterday, she'd gotten word that her apartment had been repainted and the carpet installed. They were replacing the bathroom mirror today and she could move back in anytime. She couldn't wait. She loved the hotel but staying in the space that she'd shared with Cruz was painful.

After her appointment, she intended to contact Detective Myers and let him know her plans. She planned on sleeping in her own bed tonight. And she was going to tell Scott that it wasn't necessary for Tim Burtiss to sit outside her office any longer.

When the cab parked in front of her doctor's office, Meg handed the driver a ten-dollar bill and got out. The sun was hot and she immediately felt dizzy. She balanced herself with the tips of her fingers on the sun-warmed roof of the cab and took two deeps breaths of dry, hot air. When the cab pulled away, she forced herself to walk.

The inside of the building was blissfully cool and she started to feel better. She registered at the desk and had time to read most of the current *People* magazine before the nurse called her name. When the woman weighed her, Meg was startled to realize that she'd lost three pounds.

She definitely needed to start eating better.

The nurse didn't appear concerned. "Doctor Hussein wanted us to start with some labs. Just a simple blood draw and a urine screen," she said.

CRUZ STARED AT HIS beer glass. Across the table, his long-time partner and friend, Sam Vernelli, was staring at him. "Want to talk about it?" Sam asked.

Cruz shook his head. "Nothing to talk about. You know everything. Meg had a little trouble, I tried to help, and she basically told me to pack up my stuff and take a hike. We went over this three weeks ago."

"Have you had any contact with her?"

"No." Cruz swirled the beer in his glass. "I did call Detective Myers yesterday. Unfortunately, no luck in tracking down the clothing transactions."

"It was a good idea but a long shot," Sam said. "The guy could have had the stuff in his closet for months with the tags still on."

Cruz nodded and took a sip of his beer. "I know. Myers said it's been quiet, no new threats, no new violence."

"That's good, right?" Sam asked.

Cruz shrugged. "I think so. But I have to tell you, I didn't end the call feeling much better. There was something the man wasn't saying. He was picking his words really carefully."

"What could it be?"

"I don't know. And I probably should just stop worrying about it." Cruz picked up his glass and drained it. "Meg made her choice."

"If you love her, Cruz, don't give up. Keep fighting for her. That was advice you gave me once."

And it had worked out for his partner. It was crazy to be jealous of that. Cruz forced a smile. "Speaking of your lovely wife, you better get going. Claire will be waiting."

Sam shook his head. "Her parents are in town.

Her mother wanted to help pick out the baby furniture. I'm meeting them for dinner later."

"How's Claire feeling?"

"Better now that she's a few months along. This pregnancy thing is really something."

Feeling more alone than ever, Cruz pushed back his chair and stood up. "Can't wait to see how well you do with midnight feedings and dirty diapers."

Sam stood up, too. "If my brother Jake can handle it, it can't be that tough. By the way, Joanna's pregnant again. It's a boy."

"That's great, Sam. Damn. You Vernelli boys are doing some good work." Cruz toasted Sam with his glass.

Sam leaned close. "You'll have your chance someday," he said encouragingly. "Don't think it can't happen for you."

Once again, Cruz just smiled. It was so much easier.

Pregnant.

"There must be some mistake," Meg said. She snapped and unsnapped her purse, needing to do something with the nervous energy that had exploded in her body with the doctor's announcement.

"No mistake," the doctor said. "Both the blood

test and the urine test show the same result. You're going to have a baby."

"That's impossible," Meg said.

Now the doctor frowned. "You *have* had sexual intercourse?"

Meg was feeling hot and slightly dizzy. "I… uh…well, yes. But we used birth control."

"Birth control can fail," the doctor said.

With a sudden flash, Meg remembered the first frantic sex with Cruz. The condom had come on but late in the game. "I think I need to throw up," she said. "Now."

The doctor smiled. "Of course," she said, as she handed her a small, pink plastic bucket. "Then we can talk about next steps."

A half hour later, Meg left the office with a prescription for prenatal vitamins and a whole folder full of information for the expectant parent.

She walked outside the office and realized that everything was different. The air smelled different, the warm sun felt different, the traffic sounded different. Because she was different.

She was pregnant with Cruz's child.

It was everything that she'd ever wanted but thought she could never have. And it was too much to take in.

She was scared to death.

She pulled out her cell phone. When Charlotte's

voice mail came on, she realized the woman probably wasn't back yet. "Something has come up, Charlotte. I won't be coming back to the office today."

She started walking, with no destination in mind. A half hour later, she stopped for a cup of coffee. She was the second person in line. By the time she stepped up to face the cashier, she'd changed her mind to soup and a turkey sandwich.

She needed to feed her baby.

She was responsible for another human being.

The thought of it made it difficult to move. Still, she forced herself to chew and swallow. She managed to eat most of her lunch before she pushed it away.

Terminating the pregnancy was not an option.

The idea of raising a child was terrifying.

Adoption? Could she?

She was going to have to tell Cruz. Oh, God. What would he think? Would he want the baby?

Could she stand by and let him raise their child?

How could she not? Their child deserved to have at least one parent. And he'd be a great dad. He'd been wonderful with Jana, so patient, so much fun.

He certainly wouldn't be anxious to talk to her, not after the way things had ended. But they needed to talk. Before she could lose her nerve, she pulled out her phone. The call went right to

Cruz's voice mail. With her free hand, she rubbed the sapphire necklace that she hadn't taken off since Cruz had left. Every day, under her shirt, she wore it close to her heart.

She heard the click and knew it was time to leave a message. "Cruz," she said, her throat feeling dry. "It's Meg. I…uh…have something I'd like to talk with you about. It's not an emergency or anything. But sometime, can you call me? Please."

Chapter Seventeen

Cruz was finishing a report on the latest homicide when his phone rang. He picked it up. "Montoya," he said.

"Myers here," said the caller.

"Is Meg okay?" Cruz asked, his stomach cramping up. It couldn't be good that the detective was calling him again so soon after their last conversation.

"As far as I know," he said. "Look, I've got a situation here that I need your help with."

Cruz picked up his coffee cup and took a drink. "I'm listening."

"I got a call from Debi Moulin. She said that she and her husband, Frank, had heard that you were asking questions about Troy Blakely. They have some information that you might find helpful."

"So what is it?" Cruz asked.

"That's the problem. They won't tell me. Said they would only talk to you. In person."

"Unless they're willing to get on a plane and come to Chicago, I don't see how that's going to happen."

"I told them that. I told them that you had no official capacity in this case. They said that they'd prayed about it and you were the one they could talk to. If you can be at their house at ten in the morning on Friday, they'll talk with you."

Cruz said a word that people who were prayerful didn't generally approve of. Myers laughed.

He could get the time off. That wasn't the problem. But to see Meg and know that she loved someone else, that was asking too much.

But it could put the threat to Meg to bed. And then he'd be able to stop worrying about her night and day.

Stop *thinking* about her.

Right. He needed to be satisfied with what he could get.

"Okay," Cruz said. "I'll be there." He hung up, not having any idea that the man on the other end of the line was smiling.

He realized that while he'd been talking to Myers another call had come in to his voice mail. He listened to the message, feeling his heart rate accelerate when he heard Meg's voice. *Something to talk to you about. Not an emergency.*

He hung up, feeling worse than ever.

It could only be one thing. She and Slater were getting married.

He didn't call her back. He just couldn't.

LESS THAN TWENTY-FOUR hours later, Cruz's plane landed at the San Antonio airport. He rented a car and headed toward Haileyville. At five minutes before ten, he was knocking on the Moulins' door.

Frank Moulin had salt-and-pepper hair and a belly. Cruz guessed him to be about sixty. Seconds later, when his wife joined him at the door, he realized that she was at least twenty years younger.

"I'm Cruz Montoya," he said. "I understand you wanted to talk with me."

They ushered him into their home. The rooms were small with dark paneling on the walls. The air conditioner was noisy, running on high. Frank sat in a big chair and Debi perched on the arm of the chair. Cruz sat on the sofa opposite them.

"We're not sure we want to get involved," Debi said. "But we've prayed and prayed and believe it's the right thing to do."

"You have information about Troy Blakely?"

She nodded. "We moved into the area seven years ago, after we got married. Second marriages for both of us," she added. "When Gloria Blakely learned that, she opened up to me since she was on her second marriage, too."

Debi stood up and started to pace around the room. "She was a real nice person. And she really loved Ted. But there was a sadness about her. One day, about three years ago, I saw a strange car over there. And I could hear some yelling but couldn't make out what they were saying. After the car left, I went over and she was crying something awful. She said that her son had been to see her."

Debi stopped in front of an old table, moved the lamp back a few inches, and straightened the shade. "I was surprised," she said, her back to Cruz. "I'd never heard her mention a son before. She wouldn't say much more but I got the impression that it had been some time since she'd seen the boy."

She turned and looked at Cruz. "I got her settled down and thought that was the end of it. Then that night, I heard a terrible ruckus in the middle of the night. I got up, looked out and saw somebody with a baseball bat breaking all the windows in the Blakely house."

She sat back down on the arm of her husband's chair and he put his hand on her knee. "It was him," she said. "It was the son. I saw him. I called the police."

"Did they arrest him?" Cruz asked.

"He was gone before they got here," she said.

"When they questioned me, I told them that I'd heard the noise. I didn't tell them what I saw."

"Why not?" Cruz asked.

Frank Moulin sat forward in his chair. "Because I told her not to. My wife saw the man drive away. But she saw something else, too. Gloria Blakely was standing in the front door. She knew who had done the damage. But if she wasn't going to tell the police then I didn't think we should stick our noses into it and tell them anything, either. It was a family matter."

"Did either of the Blakelys ever talk about it again?"

"No, and we didn't bring it up," Debi said. "But then Janice across the street said that you'd been here asking about them. I miss them. They were good neighbors. And I just thought it was time that somebody knew the truth."

Cruz pulled out the picture of Troy Blakely. "Was this the man that you saw?"

Debi studied the picture. A minute passed. Finally she looked up. "Well, his hair was different, but I got a real good look at his face both times and I'm sure it is the same man."

"One of your neighbors said that they thought the Blakelys might have lost a child, a little girl. Do you know anything about that?"

Debi shook her head. Frank stood up. "We've

told you everything we know. Maybe something happened in Maiter. Ted Blakely told me once that Gloria had come from there."

Maiter. Meg and Gloria Blakely had both lived there.

He left the Moulins and headed south. He thought about calling Myers but decided to wait until he knew something more concrete.

Maiter, Texas, wasn't postcard-perfect but it had the makings of a nice community. There was a main street, with mostly full storefronts. A couple restaurants, a laundry, an attorney, chiropractor and two gas stations where gas was forty cents higher a gallon than in San Antonio.

He started in one of the restaurants. It had maroon carpet, green and maroon chairs, and noisy air-conditioning that didn't seem to be working all that well. The menu was plastic, two-sided, and had at least fifty things on it, everything from spaghetti to shrimp dinners to burritos.

He ordered a hamburger and a cup of coffee and got busy checking out the possibilities. There was a table of gray-hairs, ladies in their late seventies to early eighties. They were in a corner and there was one empty chair. He wondered if it had recently just become available; they were at the age where funeral attendance became a regular event.

He figured at least a couple of them had lived

in Maiter for their whole lives. When his burger arrived, he ate quickly. Then he took a final sip of coffee, threw a bill on the table to cover lunch and approached the women.

"Ladies, could I have a minute of your time?"

They sized him up. Several smiled.

"Yes," said the woman at the end. She wore a pink button-down shirt with white slacks. She had white hair and not-very-white teeth.

"I'm trying to find an old friend. She lived here almost twenty years ago. Her name was Margaret Gunderson."

Two of the women at the far end of the table exchanged glances. One, who had a butterfly tattoo on her upper arm, narrowed her eyes but she didn't say anything.

Pink Shirt shook her head. "I don't recall anyone by that name."

The tattooed woman leaned forward. "Yes, you do, Angie. That was the girl who got in trouble at the Percy house."

Others at the table nodded. "That's right," one said. "Such a sad situation."

Trouble. Sad situation. What the hell?

He forced himself to appear relaxed. "I'm not sure I ever heard that story," he said. "If it would help me find Margaret, I'd really appreciate hearing it."

Now all eyes were on Tattoo Lady. She was evidently the team storyteller.

"Well, as I recall, it was the spring of '95 or maybe even '96. The Gundersons and the Percys were next-door neighbors, real good people. I think the husbands both worked over at the tire plant." She took a deep breath. "Yes, that's right, because the trouble continued over there."

Cruz was lost and he wanted the details straight in his head. "What trouble?"

"I'm getting to that," she said. "Margaret regularly babysat for the Percy children. She was a nice girl, very responsible."

Now that made sense.

"The baby was almost two. Real sweet and so pretty."

He nodded, hoping that she'd get to something soon that would help him.

Tattoo Lady took a sip of coffee. "Margaret made a mistake. That's all there is to it. A terrible mistake."

"What happened?" he asked, getting to the end of his patience.

"Why, she killed the baby."

Chapter Eighteen

Cruz felt the blood drain from his head. She had to be mistaken or he had to have heard it wrong. But none of the other women at the table looked shocked. They were nodding, a couple had a distant look in their eyes that suggested they were reflecting back.

"How did it happen?" he asked.

"Poor baby choked. People said Margaret got careless and left a bag of marshmallows on the table. Baby stuffed a whole bunch into her mouth and couldn't get any air. Margaret came back into the room but the poor baby was already turning blue."

Cruz had been accused by more than one perp that he didn't have a heart but at that moment he knew it wasn't true because he felt it crack in his chest. Poor Meg.

Now Pink Shirt leaned forward. "As I recall, the older boy told the police everything that had happened. Of course, he was just a child himself, can't imagine how that must have affected him."

"Were the police involved?" Cruz asked. Had Meg gone to prison?

"As I recall, there was some sort of an investigation," Pink Shirt said. "But there were no charges filed. She made a mistake. It was as simple as that."

The death of a child was never simple. Meg had carried a heavy burden. And carried it alone.

"You said something about the trouble carrying over to the tire plant?" Cruz asked.

"Mr. Percy was friends with Mr. Gunderson's supervisor. It was just months before Mr. Gunderson found himself in the street. They lost their house shortly afterward. They left town and never came back. I don't know where they ended up."

No one spoke up. Suddenly a small woman sitting in the middle sat forward in her chair. "I'm the only one at this table who has lost a child. I can tell you, it's no wonder that the Percys didn't stay together after that. Heartache changes things."

How had it changed Meg? And why had she never told him? He could feel the hamburger in his gut churning.

Pink Shirt wiped her eyes. "I thought Gloria Percy was a lovely woman. I didn't know her husband as well. I heard that she remarried a few years later but by then, I had lost touch with her. I can't even recall her husband's name."

Ted Blakely. That was his name. Gloria Percy had become Gloria Blakely. But her obituary hadn't mentioned any children.

"Whatever happened to the other child?" Cruz asked. "The brother."

"I don't know," said Tattoo Lady. "I'm not sure if T.J. ended up with his mother or his father."

T. J. Percy. "What did T.J. stand for?" Cruz asked.

The ladies looked at one another and shook their heads. "I never heard him called anything but T.J.," said Tattoo Lady.

Cruz mentally reviewed all the information he'd seen on Blakely. Nowhere had there been any mention of a middle initial or name. But he was willing to bet that the *T* stood for Troy. The boy had stayed with his mother and taken his stepfather's last name. T. J. Percy had become Troy Blakely.

And something had happened to set him off, to make him seek vengeance on Meg. It had probably been his mother's and stepfather's deaths. The timing was right. He'd somehow managed to track Meg down, realized she was in San Antonio, and had gotten the job at the hotel. He'd lost it just months later. Maybe that had made him even angrier. Maybe he hadn't cared. After all, he'd already learned Meg's routine, had copied the key to her office, figured out where she parked. Followed her home.

The vision of a man breaking all the windows in his mother's house as she looked on made the blood in Cruz's veins run cold. What kind of son did that to his parents? A crazy man. Maybe he'd been crazy for some time. Certainly somewhere along the way, something had gone south in the Blakely house. To the point that Gloria and Ted Blakely didn't even claim T.J. as their son.

The women were all staring at him. He wasn't sure how long he'd been standing at the head of the table, trying to figure out the whole horrid mess.

"Thank you," he managed.

"Would you like to join us for a piece of pie, young man?" Pink Shirt asked. She pointed to the empty chair.

He shook his head. He didn't need pie. He needed air. To clear his head so that he could figure out what to do next.

There was no need for panic, he rationalized. Nothing had happened for weeks. Meg wasn't in any more danger today than she had been yesterday, the day before, or last week. Maybe much less. Blakely could well have tired of the game and moved on.

Of course, Cruz was going to make sure of that.

And by the time he got back to his hot car, he had a plan. Blakely's mother and stepfather were dead. But that still left his biological father. He might know where his son was hanging out.

Cruz pushed a button on his cell phone. Sam answered on the third ring.

"I need some more help," Cruz said.

"Name it," Sam said.

"I need to find somebody. A man by the last name of Percy. He lived in Maiter, Texas, in 1995 or 1996. He was married to a woman named Gloria. They had a son whose name was Troy and also a deceased infant girl. Her name was Missy. They got divorced and the wife later remarried a man named Ted Blakely."

"Okay, it's probably enough. I'll find him."

It took Sam twenty minutes. Computers were wonderful things. Lawrence Percy had been twenty miles outside San Antonio for the past ten years. He was single and he had steadily been employed as a machinist in a factory.

Cruz put his now-cool car in Drive.

LAWRENCE PERCY ANSWERED his door wearing sloppy sweatpants and a stained T-shirt. His hair had specks of green paint in it. He was holding a brush. "Yeah?" he asked.

Cruz immediately decided a direct approach might work best. "I'm Detective Cruz Montoya.

I'm investigating a series of events that occurred in San Antonio."

The man blinked once. "I don't go into the city." He moved to shut the door.

Cruz stuck an arm out. "Margaret Gunderson," he said.

The man's jaw dropped. "I haven't heard that name in a long time," he said, his voice soft.

Cruz considered and took a chance. "She's my ex-wife."

The man's eyes turned watery. "How is she?"

It wasn't the response Cruz expected. "I wasn't sure you'd care. I recently heard the story about your child's death."

The man nodded. "I was so angry with her. Hated her. She was alive, walking down our street and our sweet Missy would never get that chance. I wanted her to suffer. I wanted her whole family to pay."

"Past tense?" Cruz questioned. "You still want her to suffer?"

The man shook his head. "No. She suffered enough. We all did."

"Why did you leave Maiter?"

"My son, T.J., was struggling in school. Moving didn't help. Nothing did."

"What's your son's full name?"

"Troy Jamison."

"Where is your son now?"

"I have no idea. For a while, he moved in and out of my mother's house in San Antonio. They'd get along for a while, then there'd be some big blowup. But she always took him back. 'He's my blood,' she would say." The man's eyes turned bleak. "I had to turn my back on my own mother. Haven't seen either of them for over five years."

"What's your mother's address?"

The man hesitated. "What's going on?"

"Someone is terrorizing Meg. Trashing her car, her apartment, her office. Following her. I think it could be your son. For a brief period, he worked at the same hotel that Meg works at. I think that was on purpose."

The man didn't look surprised. "Got a pen?" he asked. Then he rattled off the address. Cruz wrote it down.

"Thank you," Cruz said. "Again, I'm sorry for your loss."

Lawrence Percy nodded. "Be careful. I don't know my son all that well anymore but I suspect he could be very dangerous. The only thing I really know for sure is that I wish to hell he wasn't my blood."

CRUZ DIALED MEG as he ran for the car. It went to voice mail. "Meg," he said, "be careful. It's Troy Blakely. Watch out for him."

The next call he made was to Detective Myers. When he answered, Cruz gave him just enough details for the man to understand the urgency of the situation. The detective said he was an hour outside San Antonio but that he'd leave immediately for the hotel.

Cruz was half that. He drove fast, trying to shave another few minutes. He tried Meg's office again and got the same busy signal. He pressed zero and got bounced back to the hotel operator who transferred him to Charlotte's desk.

It rang and rang. He went through the whole routine again with the operator, but this time he asked to be transferred to Security, hoping they could get a message to Tim Burtiss.

He got voice mail again.

Damn it. Did no one answer their phones anymore?

He glanced at his watch. He'd be there in fifteen minutes. He forced himself to calm down. Everything would be fine.

MEG WAS ON A LONG CALL with a disgruntled guest when a note slid under her closed office door. When she finished the call a few minutes later, she walked over and picked it up. It was from Charlotte. *Scott called. He wants to see you right away.*

Meg crumpled up the note and tossed it in her

waste can. After learning about the baby, she'd gone to see Scott. Hadn't told him about the pregnancy. Cruz deserved to hear that news first. But she had told him that she was sorry. Sorry that she'd involved him in her deceit, that he was a good man who deserved better. He'd read between the lines and had made it easy for her by saying all the right things. *I respect you. I care for you. Of course we can still work together.*

Hopefully, he hadn't changed his mind about that. She needed an income and health insurance.

She looked at her phone and saw that there was a voice mail waiting. She decided to ignore it. She'd see what Scott needed first and then get to her calls. She grabbed a yellow legal pad and hurried out.

When she opened the door that connected her office to Charlotte's, she saw that the space was empty. She opened the outer door and the security guard sprang to his feet.

"Have you seen Charlotte?" she asked.

"No. I thought she was at her desk."

She must have left by the other door. Maybe she had to use the restroom and didn't want to announce it to the security guard. "No problem. She probably just stepped out for a minute. When she comes back, let her know that I saw her note and that I'm in Mr. Slater's office."

"I'll walk you," he said.

There hadn't been any issues for weeks. But the memory of her destroyed office still nagged at her. She could lock it but didn't know if Charlotte had her keys. "Just stay here," she said. "It's just up the elevator. Nothing is going to happen between here and there."

She walked down the hallway, took the elevator to the next floor, and was fifteen feet away from Scott's office when a door opened and a man stepped out. She saw his eyes first. They were dark and cold. She saw the gun next—it was black and deadly looking.

"Keep walking, Meg," he muttered. "Don't make any sudden moves or I'll shoot you here. Then I'm going to shoot anybody who comes running to help."

Chapter Nineteen

Meg's mind scrambled to make sense of it. "What do you want?"

The man didn't answer. Just pointed her toward the stairs.

She went. *Stupid. Stupid. Stupid.* It was all she could think of. Cruz would be so damn disappointed in her. He was so smart, so careful and she'd been so careless.

What would he tell her to do now?

Stay alert. Figure out who he is and what he wants. Be smart. She could practically feel heat coming off the sapphire necklace, burning her skin.

They reached the landing at the bottom. She looked up, hoping the camera would catch a good view of her face. It had been knocked down. "What do you want?" she asked again.

"Shut up," he said. He poked her in the back with his gun. "My car is twenty feet from this door. Walk directly to it and get in the driver's side. Don't be stupid."

It was a blue four-door with tinted windows. When she opened the door, the smell of smoke rolled out at her. It made her want to throw up. She swallowed hard and got in. He slid into the back-seat. He tossed the keys over the seat, into her lap and pressed the gun against her neck.

"Drive. Turn left onto Bridge Street."

Her hands were shaking so badly that she couldn't get the key into the ignition. She took a deep breath and was immediately sorry when the horrible smell traveled farther into her lungs.

She finally got the car started and pulled out of the lot. They drove for fifteen minutes, turning this way and that on busy city streets. She tried to keep track of where she was but it was an area of the city that she wasn't familiar with. Finally, he directed her to turn onto a street where the apartment buildings were close together and run-down. "Right there," he said, pointing to an empty parking spot.

It was a tight fit, even for the small car. She put the vehicle in Park and shut off the engine. It was stone-quiet in the car. And the oppressive heat from outside seeped in.

She could hear him pulling off his face mask. "Get out," he said. "We're going into that build-ing," he said, pointing at a six-story structure that had several broken-out windows.

The front door of the building looked as if someone had tried to kick it in. It was dented and beat up and didn't close quite right. She opened it and he pushed her toward the stairs. "Keep walking," he said. On the fourth floor, he yanked her back and pointed to a door at the end of the hallway. He unlocked the door and they stepped inside a small, filthy apartment. There were dirty dishes, empty food boxes and trash everywhere. It smelled like cat urine. There was a table in the middle of the kitchen, long and narrow, with a wood top that was scratched and pitted. On it were guns, probably half a dozen, all in some half-state of assembly. There was a can of gun oil and dirty rags.

She turned to look at him. He was only a couple inches taller than her and had a slim build. He wore dirty army fatigues.

His hair was bleached blond and touched his shoulders. He had a straggly blond mustache. While there was little resemblance to the man she'd known, who had worn his dark hair and beard trimmed short and always had a pressed uniform, there was no doubt. He was Troy Blakely.

All this time, Cruz had been on the right track.

And with his hair blond and more of his bone structure visible, she saw something else that she recognized.

Her world started to go gray and she grabbed for the table behind her.

"It's been a long time, Meg," he said.

A very long time. "Hello, T.J."

CRUZ BEACHED HIS CAR in the valet parking, ignoring the yells from the startled valets. He ran into the hotel, through the lobby, toward Meg's office.

Tim Burtiss stood. "I didn't know you were back, sir."

"Where's Meg?" Cruz asked.

"Mr. Slater's office," Tim answered.

Cruz took off running again, taking the steps to the third floor two at a time. When he got to Slater's office, the receptionist wasn't at her desk. He opened the inner-office door and Slater looked up from his desk.

"Where's Meg?" Cruz asked.

"Get out," Slater said.

"Where is she?" Cruz asked.

Slater shrugged his shoulders. "I have no idea. I haven't talked to her all morning."

Cruz got a very bad feeling. "Come with me," he said. "Something is not right."

To Slater's credit, he didn't argue. Just hurried down the hall with Cruz. When they got back to Meg's office, Officer Burtiss stood again.

"Is Meg back?" Cruz asked hopefully.

"No, sir. Neither she nor Charlotte have returned."

They were both missing? What the hell did Charlotte have to do with this?

Cruz opened the door. He searched Charlotte's work area first. The light was on, as was her computer and there was a cup of coffee on her desk. Cruz felt the cup. Still warm.

He moved into Meg's office. There was a yellow legal pad on her desk, filled with pages of notes. He glanced at them. Some kind of customer complaint. He pointed at the name. "See if this guest is still here," he instructed Slater. Was it possible that Meg had simply left to personally resolve a problem?

While Slater was on the phone, Cruz kept looking. He saw the crumpled up note in Meg's garbage and unfolded it. He read it.

Slater ended his call. "They checked out two days ago."

Cruz showed the note to Slater. "You didn't talk to Charlotte this morning?"

"No. What the hell is going on here?"

Cruz looked at Meg's phone. He saw the voice mail light blinking and realized it was probably his frantic message. "I don't know. But we need to find both of them." He pulled out his cell phone to call Myers and fill him in. Before he dialed, he continued his instructions. "The police will be here soon. Get your security staff started on searching the hotel. Tell them to hurry."

"T.J.," SHE SAID, working hard to keep her voice steady. She did not want him to know that her sudden knowledge had her insides twisting up in a painful knot.

He ran a hand through his long hair. "I hated having to cut my hair for that stupid job. And the beard itched like hell. But nobody would have ever known it. Because I was nice. Officer Friendly, that was me." He laughed at his own joke. "Yes, Ms. Montoya. No, Ms. Montoya. Whatever you want, Ms. Montoya."

"I'm sorry I didn't recognize you," she said, staring at his light brown eyes. Without the glasses and the blue eyes, it was easier to recognize him.

He laughed again. It was almost a cackle and it made him sound crazy. "Blue contacts. Weren't they fabulous? I'll bet you are sorry. I watched you every day and you had no idea."

"How did you find me?"

"I went through my mother's filing cabinet after she and my stepfather died. She had a copy of your wedding announcement. Once I had your married name, it wasn't hard to find you, although I never expected you to be in Texas."

He sprawled onto the dirty couch and motioned for her to sit in the lone straight-backed kitchen chair. "You're some kind of big shot. You get your picture in the paper and everything." He tilted his head down. "You know why you help convicts, Meg? Because you almost were one. They should have sent you to jail for what you did."

She wasn't sure what to say to that. "I'm sorry you lost your job at the hotel," she said, searching for some way to turn him. "I could talk with our human resources manager and you could get it back. Start fresh."

"I already told you it was a crappy job." He got up and started to pace around her.

Okay. That probably wasn't the right tactic. "How are your parents?" she asked.

He stopped suddenly. "My mommy is dead," he said, as if he was five years old.

The hair on the back of her neck stood up. "I'm sorry to hear that, T.J."

"Don't call me that," he yelled, lunging at her. He got so close that his spit hit her face. "You ruined everything. We lost everything because of you."

"I was fifteen," she said. "I'm sorry."

"It doesn't matter," he said. "Now, you're going

to pay." He kicked her chair, hard enough that it pushed her backward. "You sit right there," he said. "Don't move."

She did as he instructed. And she took deep breaths, trying to quiet her racing heart. *Be smart. Be smarter than he is.*

"Everybody loves Meg," he said, in a singsong voice. "Even my own Nana. She tried to warn you. Said I was wrong to hate so much." He gave her a big smile. "A couple days ago I gave her a taste of what would happen if she didn't keep her mouth shut. Made sure she told the doctor she fell down the steps. Old ladies and broken hips don't do so well together."

She remembered Grandma Percy. She'd been the only Percy to offer any comfort to Meg. Had seemed to understand that Meg was as devastated as a person could be and still be standing. She'd been kind. And she'd doted on T.J.

Tried to warn you. It had to have been her that had come to Meg's office. And he'd hurt her.

She wanted to strike out, to punch him as hard as she could, but she thought of her baby and kept her arms hanging loosely at her sides.

DETECTIVE MYERS BROUGHT a whole team to search the hotel. It paid off because they found Charlotte tied up, with duct tape across her mouth, in the fourth-floor janitor closet.

They peeled off the tape and she started spewing.

"He made me write the note. Said that he would kill me if I didn't. Said he would kill my mother, too."

"Who?" Cruz demanded.

"That crazy guy who used to work in security. He looked different but I recognized him. Blakely. Troy Blakely. Is Meg okay?"

Cruz couldn't answer.

"We don't know," Detective Myers said.

"I'm sorry. He told me what I had to write on the note and then watched me as I slid it under the door. Then we went out the side door and came up here. He opened the door, told me to come inside and tied me up. I tried screaming and that's when he put the duct tape over my mouth."

Myers looked at Cruz. "We'll find him."

"You better find her fast," Charlotte said, looking at Slater. "She's pregnant."

Cruz felt like he'd taken a punch in the stomach. He balled up his fist and turned toward Slater.

Slater held up his hand. "We *never* had that kind of relationship. Look, Meg doesn't love me. She made that perfectly clear just last night. We're not together. We've never been together and we never will be. She's still in love with you."

Cruz's legs felt weak. He grabbed hold of a shelf to steady himself. Slater might be a jerk but he had always cared for Meg. He wouldn't lie about something like this. And while his brain was processing that, it was also snapping with the realization that he and Meg had had exactly that kind of relationship. About a month ago. Holy hell.

Charlotte's eyes filled with tears. She reached out for Slater's hand. "I thought it was your baby. I hated her for that." She turned to look at Cruz. "But I never would have hurt her."

Cruz waved away the explanation. "How do you know she's pregnant?"

The woman's fair face turned pink. "I took my mother to the doctor and when we were leaving, I saw Meg leaving her doctor's office. Early this morning, I saw a prescription for prenatal vitamins on her desk."

I have something I need to tell you. It's not an emergency.

Like hell it wasn't. "Let's go," he said, looking at Myers. Meg was pregnant with his child and they were both in danger.

"Where?" Myers asked.

"I have his grandmother's address, here in San Antonio. I'm hoping she can tell us something."

They took Myers's car and used both the lights and siren to speed around traffic. The house was a small ranch on a well-maintained street. There was no garage and no car in the narrow driveway.

Cruz ran up the sidewalk and knocked sharply on the front door. He waited twenty seconds and knocked again. Louder.

Myers stepped off the front porch and started looking in windows. The horizontal blinds were down but they were tilted enough to make the interior visible.

"Anything?" Cruz asked, knocking a third time.

"Nope. No lights on inside. Can't see a whole lot but the place looks empty."

Just then the front door of a neighboring house opened. A woman, probably in her late sixties, stepped onto the porch. "Can I help you?" she asked.

Myers stepped forward and flashed his badge. "We're looking for Mrs. Percy."

The woman shook her head sadly. "You'll have to go to Lakeview Hospital. She was taken there by ambulance two days ago."

"What happened?"

"She broke her hip. *Said* she fell down her basement steps."

Cruz stepped forward. "You say that as if you don't believe it."

The woman shrugged. "I'm not accusing anybody of anything. All I'm saying is that Loretta Percy has been living in that house for twelve years and she's never fallen down the basement stairs. But the one time her grandson visits, it happens. That seems like an odd coincidence to me."

Cruz started running for the car. He could hear Myers on his heels. They made it to the hospital in less than fifteen minutes. They asked to speak to a charge nurse and they were quickly escorted into Loretta Percy's room.

The woman was banged up. She had bruises and cuts on her face and arms. The rest of her body was covered by a sheet. Her eyes were closed.

"Mrs. Percy," Cruz said, trying to keep the edge out of his voice.

The woman opened her eyes. "Yes," she said.

"I'm Detective Cruz Montoya. I'm looking for your grandson, Troy Blakely."

"What did he do?" she asked, her voice weak.

"I think he has my wife. Margaret Gunderson."

The woman closed her eyes and seemed to shrink in her bed. "I'm sorry," she said. "She's a good girl."

"We need to know where he is. Do you have any idea?"

She shook her head. "He lived with me up until a year ago. He changed after his mother died. They had had a big argument a few years back. He was very upset that they hadn't reconciled before she died. My grandson has a tendency to blame others for his troubles. After his mother died, he became fixated on your wife. He said that everything that went wrong in his life started with her."

Myers stepped forward. "Did he do this?" he asked.

The woman didn't answer.

"Did you go to Meg Montoya's office?" Myers asked. "To tell her about Troy?"

The woman nodded and licked her dry lips. "I could see that he was getting worse. All he talked about was that Meg had to pay for the trouble she'd caused. If it helps, he has my car. It's a blue Ford Focus, a 2005." She reached for the tablet and pen that was on the narrow tray table that swiveled over her bed. "Here's the license plate number." She shifted her eyes to Cruz. "You better find her fast."

Chapter Twenty

It took Myers less than a minute to get the word out. Every cop on the street was going to be looking for the car.

"Now what?" Myers asked.

"We're going back to the only place I know that he's been to recently."

It took them twelve minutes. The front door was locked and the restaurant was dark inside. It wouldn't be open for several hours. "Back door?" Myers asked.

Cruz led the way through the alley. He didn't bother to knock on the screen door, just pushed it open and walked into the kitchen. There were two men, one stirring something in a big pot, the other cutting up raw chicken. They started yelling in some foreign language.

Myers flashed his badge and they got quiet.

"We don't want to cause you any trouble," Cruz said. "I'm looking for the woman who waitresses here. Thin. Blond hair. Thirties. I want her name and address."

The two men looked at each other. The man cutting up the chicken gave the other a curt nod. The man stirring the soup stopped.

"Abby Breese. She lives just down the street, in the three-story building at the corner."

The man's English was pretty good. Cruz nodded his thanks and took off running. He could hear Myers behind him. The building was old, dirty and smelled bad. There was carpet in the foyer that had likely been there twenty years.

The scratched and dented mailboxes at the entrance indicated that A. Breese lived on the third floor. Cruz ran up all three flights. He knocked sharply and waited impatiently. Finally, the door opened.

It was the woman he was looking for. She didn't look surprised to see him and he figured one of the guys from the restaurant had called to warn her.

"Detective Montoya," she said.

"I want to know if you've recently seen Troy Blakely. It's important."

She stared at Cruz. "He's done something bad, hasn't he?" she asked.

Cruz hoped not. "I don't know."

"I saw him earlier this week."

"At the restaurant."

"Yes. He stopped for food. I asked him where he was living and he said that he'd moved to an apartment in the Valdez area."

"Street?" Cruz demanded.

She shook her head. "He said he was getting lots of exercise because he was on the fourth floor."

"HURTING ME ISN'T going to bring Missy back," Meg said.

T.J. shook his head. "I don't care about Missy. I never did. I hated her. Always crying and getting all the attention."

Missy had been a good baby. She'd hardly ever been fussy. And she'd idolized her big brother. Tried to follow him everywhere, be just like him. If T.J. wanted hot dogs for lunch, then that's what Missy wanted.

He could do no wrong.

Except that one time. With a chill, Meg remembered walking into the family room, expecting to see T.J. and Missy watching a movie and instead, had seen T.J. with a toy gun in his hands, shooting Missy's collection of dolls that he'd lined up across the room.

Missy had been sitting on the couch, tears running down her face.

Meg had gathered up the guns, put the dolls safely back on Missy's shelves and told T.J. that he couldn't ever do something like that again. She'd mentioned it to Gloria and the gun had disappeared by the next time she went over to babysit.

"You don't want to go to prison, T.J. That's what will happen if you hurt me," she said. "It's not too late. We can undo this."

"I hated you, too," he said. He ran his hands through his hair, pulling at it. He started to sway from side to side. "You loved Missy more, just like everyone else."

"I didn't," she said. She glanced past him. If she could get around the couch, she might make it to the door before he could stop her. "I'm sorry you thought that."

He ignored the apology. "But I figured out a way to get both of you," he said. He was swaying so fast, it looked as if he were rocking. "It was easy, too. I heard the doorbell ring and knew that you'd gone to answer the door. I wanted ice cream but I sure as hell wasn't asking you for anything. I saw her sitting in her highchair with the marshmallows at the other end of the table. I wanted some. I ate one and she started to cry. I didn't want you coming back so I gave her a bunch. She stuffed them all in her mouth. Her cheeks were full of them. She was stupid. Couldn't even figure out how to swallow."

He abruptly stopped rocking and started pacing

around her in circles. "She started to turn blue. I knew I'd get the blame. I always got the blame for everything. So I loosened up the tray on the highchair, pulled her out and sat her on the table, next to the bag of marshmallows. Then I went back into the other room and started watching television again." He lifted one corner of his mouth in an ugly sneer. "When the police came, you told them that I'd been watching television the whole time. You made it so easy for everyone to blame you."

Meg put a hand to her throat, pressing down the urge to vomit. She hadn't been careless. She hadn't caused sweet Missy's death. He had. All these years. All the guilt.

Leaving Cruz.

Being afraid to have her own child.

She had never been so angry in her whole life.

Or so determined. She needed to save her baby, save herself. And T.J. was obviously crazy. Earlier he'd been blaming her for all his family's troubles when he clearly knew that he'd caused all the havoc. She didn't need to convince him that she hadn't done anything wrong; he knew. "I always hoped I'd see you again," she said. "I had some pictures of your mother. Of her and you together that I wanted to give you."

His head jerked up. She'd caught his attention.

"Where?" he demanded.

Given that he'd been in both her apartment and her office, those weren't good options. "I have a safe deposit box at the bank. I keep all my important papers there."

"Which bank?"

"The one across from the hotel," she said. "I have the key in my purse," she said. "Back at the office. Of course, it won't do you much good. Banks are really strict about who gets access. If your name isn't on the list, it doesn't matter whether you have a key or not."

He started to rock again. "How many pictures?" he asked.

"I don't recall for sure. But I know there were several and they were really good shots. I think one of them was of your mom and you sitting on your front porch. Remember when you used to do that?"

He didn't answer. Sweat was running down his face. Without saying another word, he picked up his phone. He pushed a button, putting it on speaker. Then he connected to directory assistance. "Fillmore Federal in San Antonio," he said. While the operator was connecting the call, he pointed a finger at her. "Get them to verify that you've got a safe deposit box there or you'll be dead before they hang up the phone."

Meg swallowed hard. When the bank answered, she asked to be transferred to the safe deposit department.

"Hi," she said. "This is Margaret Montoya calling. I'm a little embarrassed to be making this call but I relocated to San Antonio within the last year and opened accounts at two different banks. I also opened a safe deposit box at one bank but I can't quite remember which bank." She laughed nervously. "Would you be able to tell me if I have a safe deposit box at your bank?"

The woman at the other end chuckled. "I'm glad I'm not the only one who forgets things." There was a pause. "Yes, Ms. Montoya. Your safe deposit box is with us."

Meg looked at T.J. He was breathing so hard that it almost seemed as if he was panting. "Thank you so much," Meg said. "What are your hours today?"

"We're open until four," the woman said.

"Thanks again," Meg said, and hung up. Four. They closed in less than fifteen minutes. The ride from the hotel to the apartment had taken at least that. There was no time to get it today.

"We need that key. Damn it," he added, as he slammed his fist into the wall. Meg tried not to flinch. She'd managed to get a tiny bit of leverage. She didn't want him to realize that she was so frightened that she could barely breathe.

"We're going back to the hotel tonight. And you're going to get your safe deposit key," he said. "Then tomorrow, we're going to the bank. If you do anything stupid, a lot of people will die."

There would be multiple opportunities for escape. She would find one and end this, before anyone got hurt because of her. She could not live with that again.

"Sit there," he said, motioning for her to move from her chair to the couch.

She shook her head. "I can sit here," she said.

"Move, damn it," he yelled and he pointed his gun at her.

She got up. She would survive this. She would have to. Her baby's life depended upon it.

She sat on the couch, near the armrest, and he crouched next to her. The next thing happened so fast, so unexpectedly, that she yelped when a cold, black steel manacle snapped around her wrist.

She looked down. Anchoring her in place was a thick metal chain connected to a bolt that was drilled into the old wood floor. She was trapped, like an animal in a cage.

Chapter Twenty-One

Meg bit her lip. She would not beg or cry. She would not give him the satisfaction. She would simply endure.

He surprised her when he backed away and pulled out the lone metal chair that sat at one end of the narrow table. He sat, his left side toward her. She watched as he picked up a gun, cradled it in one hand and gently rubbed it with a rag.

He didn't say another word to her. Sometime later, maybe forty minutes or so, she saw one of his hands drift down below the table and he stroked himself through his pants. Her breath caught in her chest. She wanted to look away but she was frozen.

It went on for some minutes before he pushed back his chair and walked into the small bathroom. He shut the door but the wood was thin and the gap between the door and the floor significant. The sounds from the small room told the story.

A minute after he *finished,* the door opened.

He didn't look at her. He picked up the sleeping bag that hung on the back of the door, untied the strings, unrolled it onto the dirty carpet and lay down. He was asleep in minutes.

She had to pee but even if she could have gotten up, she didn't think she would ever ask to use that bathroom. She would hold it until she exploded.

She couldn't sleep. Not after what T.J. had told her. Everything she believed for years had changed and her mind was whirling.

Melissa Ann Percy. Everybody had called her Missy. And everybody had loved her, especially Meg. She'd been the little sister that Meg had always wanted. And whenever the Percys had called her to babysit, she'd jumped at the chance.

Mrs. Percy had always dressed her daughter like a little doll, in sweet dresses with matching tights. Missy's blond hair had natural curls and she was forever losing the barrettes that Gloria insisted she start the day with.

A half hour before Missy died, Meg had run the bath water. It was the middle of July and Missy had been sweaty and dirty from playing outside. Meg could still feel the weight of the little girl's body as she picked her up and swung her over the edge of the white tub. She'd soaped her up and Missy had giggled and squirmed and when she was all rinsed off, Meg had wrapped her wet naked body in a big towel.

She'd smelled so good.

Meg had dressed her in her favorite pajamas, the ones with little pigs running across them. And she'd brushed the tangles out of her hair. And she'd said yes when the little girl had begged for a treat before bedtime.

She'd been big enough to crawl up into her highchair and she'd raised her little arms, impatient for Meg to attach the tray. Then she'd grinned when Meg had pulled a bag of marshmallows out of the cupboard. They were her favorite.

Meg had given her one and watched her eat it. Then another. And then the doorbell had rung.

It was almost eight-thirty and close to dark. But she hadn't been scared. Maiter wasn't Houston, where Meg's family had always double-checked to make sure their windows and doors were locked. It was the kind of place where kids slept out in the backyard in tents and teenagers hung around the park at night after the summer baseball game had ended, talking and maybe sneaking the occasional cigarette.

Everybody knew everybody. And while some teenage girls might have been bored in the little town, Meg had been glad that her dad had lost his job in Houston and they'd moved to Maiter.

Otherwise, she'd have never met the Percys who lived across the street in the big white house. She'd never have met Missy.

She'd gone to answer the door and it had been Mrs. Moore, the woman who lived next door. The Percys had been collecting her mail while she'd been out of town visiting her mother and she'd come to get it. Meg had retrieved it off the big dining room table, chatted for just a minute, and closed the heavy door after the woman.

And then she'd gone back into the kitchen. And sweet Missy had been lying on the kitchen table, her lips blue.

Not breathing.

The open bag of marshmallows was next to her, with more spilled out on the table.

Meg had grabbed her, stuck her fingers in her mouth, and swept out half-chewed marshmallows. But she remained unresponsive. Meg had looked up and T.J. was standing in the doorway, between the kitchen and living room, his eyes wide. "Stay here," Meg had yelled and she'd run out of the house into the night, the little girl in her arms, screaming for help.

Hours later, when it had all been over, and she'd been sitting at her own kitchen table, listening to the police talk to her parents, she'd heard them say "lodged in her windpipe, just like a cork."

The small town, the one that she'd started to really like, was no longer friendly and welcoming. Because everywhere she went, she was the girl who let sweet Missy Percy choke to death.

But she hadn't.

For years she'd relived every moment of that night, breaking each action into discreet moments. She'd heard the click of the tray snapping onto the highchair, hadn't she? She'd only talked to the neighbor for a minute, right?

It drove her crazy.

In the end, she'd realized it didn't matter. Missy was dead. The Percys had lost a daughter. T.J. had lost a sister.

She had lost everyone's trust. She'd disappointed the people who loved her most.

Now, she stared at Troy Blakely and felt as if she wanted to jump out of her own skin. She hated. For the first time in her life, she knew that she honestly hated.

Intellectually, on a better day, she knew that she might be able to reason that he was a sick man. Had obviously been a sick child. But she could not bring herself to feel sorry for him.

No. She felt sorry for his parents. At what point did they know that they had raised a monster? At what point did they stop thinking about their little girl? They never got to see her first day of kindergarten, her first high school dance, her college graduation. They never again got to feel her chubby arms wrap around their necks. They never got to kiss her good-night and stroke her soft hair.

Her own parents had suffered, too. She could still remember sitting on the top step in the dark, weeks after Missy's death, listening to her parents talk in the downstairs living room. Her father had been loudest. *How could she have been so careless?* Her mother's voice softer but no less filled with despair. *I don't know.*

A month later, after her father had lost his job, she'd tried to tell them how sorry she was. She'd cried and they'd told her that they still loved her. Her mother had patted her hand. *We will never talk about this again.*

And she hadn't.

But she had thought about it every day for the past twenty years. And she had grieved.

MYERS'S TEAM IDENTIFIED twenty-nine buildings that had four or more stories in the eight-block area known as Valdez. It was called that because it surrounded Valdez Park, where a small statue marked the contributions of some hero from the Spanish-American war. The park might have been nice at one time but now it was run-down, matching the apartment buildings that lined the streets.

At least half of them had more than ten floors and six had more than twenty floors. It was a hell of a lot of space to cover.

Myers started by calling in the canine unit. Four dogs and their handlers arrived within the half hour. They got a shirt out of Meg's dirty laundry pile and the dogs picked up her scent. The officers, twelve in total, split into four teams of three. Each team took a dog and they started working the list. Cruz was grateful for the manpower. He realized it was probably every available cop that they could spare. He and Myers paired up, making a fifth team. They didn't have a dog but Cruz didn't intend to let that stop him.

The plan was fairly simple. Knock on doors, ask a few questions, show both Blakely's and Meg's pictures, and let the dog do his thing. If the animal showed any interest, investigate further. If not, move on. Any leads or new information would immediately get triaged back to the temporary command center that had been set up unobtrusively in a trailer in an empty parking lot.

Fortunately, the neighborhood was one that the police knew well in that there was frequent violence requiring a police response. They were on a first-name basis with lots of people in the community. Even so, some doors went unanswered. A few of the inhabitants might have been working but many more were likely inside but just not keen on interacting with the police.

They didn't break down any doors. If they couldn't get inside to do a visual, they relayed that information back to one additional officer who was charged with tracking down landlords, to get access through them.

Nobody recognized Blakely or Meg.

As report after report funneled into Myers, Cruz got more worried. Meg. Sweet Meg. Who could only see the good in people. How would she handle a crazy man?

Stay alive, Meg. Just stay alive until I can find you. Keep our baby safe.

Their baby. It was staggering news. Wonderful news. Terrifying news in these circumstances.

Meg had tried to tell him. Why the hell hadn't he returned her call? Why the hell had he let his pride get in the way?

Eight hours later, it was just past midnight and the streetlights in the area that hadn't been broken out had been burning for over four hours.

Cruz and Myers had been moving at a relentless pace. Ten minutes ago, Myers had insisted they return to the command center and he'd pushed a turkey sandwich and a cup of coffee into Cruz's hands. "Eat," he said. "Before you fall down."

Cruz gulped down the food. He was wadding

up his sandwich wrapper when he glanced down the street. Two blocks away, he saw a man and a woman emerge from a building. They were moving fast, the man had his arm around the woman. The angle of the streetlight was just right and holy hell, he couldn't be sure it was Meg but he'd caught a glimpse of rich, dark hair.

Cruz grabbed Myers's arm, pointed and ran for his car. He had the car started and was pulling away when Myers wrenched open the passenger-side door and slid in. The man started talking into his radio, giving other officers their location. It took four blocks before Cruz's vehicle and two other unmarked cars converged around the blue Focus.

There was enough light to see that it was Blakely and Meg and the bastard had a gun pointed at her head. She was alert and watchful and he willed her to stay calm, to not give the man any reason to shoot.

Stand down. Myers got the message to his team.

"How long to get a sniper to take him out?" Cruz asked, his voice low.

"Five minutes."

Cruz pulled his gun. Myers looked at it, frowned, but didn't say a word.

While five minutes wasn't a long time, it was too long because Blakely decided to move. He opened his car door. "Don't come any closer or I'll kill her," he yelled.

"Nobody needs to get hurt, Mr. Blakely," Myers yelled back. "Let Meg go and we can talk about this."

"We have to go to the bank," Blakely yelled.

Myers looked at Cruz. *What the hell?*

Cruz shook his head. It was the middle of the night.

"Okay. Let Meg go and we'll take you to the bank," Myers said.

"She has to go, too." Blakely sounded frantic. Cruz could see that the hand that held the gun was shaking. "First to the hotel, then to the bank. You get someone to open the bank now."

"Okay, okay," Myers said. "We'll get in touch with the manager right now and see if he can come down and unlock the doors." He turned to Cruz. "I want both of them out of that car. It's a better shot for our sniper."

Cruz didn't answer. He judged the distance, angled his body and raised his gun. He didn't intend to wait.

"Continue to stand down," Myers instructed the other officers. "You, too," he said to Cruz.

Cruz ignored him. He focused on Blakely and tried to keep his eyes off Meg. He couldn't look at her pinched, tight face or focus on the fear in her eyes.

She'd always been his weakness and now more so than ever. His child's life also hung in the balance. Without them, he was nothing.

"Damn you, Montoya," Myers said. "Don't make me take that gun away from you."

Cruz continued to ignore him. Blakely was moving, pulling Meg out of the car. He grabbed her around the waist and hauled her in front of him, using her as a human shield. He was only a few inches taller, not leaving a whole lot of room for error on the sniper's part.

It had the potential to end very badly.

Cruz took a breath.

"Hurl," he yelled.

A fraction of a second delay, then Meg bent at the waist. Cruz fired. His shot hit Blakely in the shoulder, knocking him back.

The two closest officers sprang forward and tackled him. Meg ran.

Cruz caught her before she'd gone ten feet. He swung her up in his arms, buried his face in her hair and breathed in the scent of life. For a long moment, he could not speak. "I thought I'd lost you," he finally managed.

"I'm so sorry," Meg said, pulling her head back. "I wasn't as careful as I should have been."

"It doesn't matter. None of it matters. It's over."

She was shaking and he held her close. Finally, she lifted her eyes. "I have something to tell you."

"Okay," he said.

"I'm pregnant."

He brushed her hair back from her face. "I know. Charlotte told me. It's a long story that I'll tell you sometime."

"Are you mad?" she asked.

"Honey, I'm thrilled. I want you. I want our child. I want it all."

Her eyes filled with tears. "I wanted you to have it all," she said. "That's why I left."

He nodded. "That's what I figured. I'm sorry that little girl died. But it was just an accident. You can't blame yourself."

"It wasn't an accident. It was T.J."

He had all kinds of questions but now wasn't the time. "Can you put it behind you?" he asked.

"I will never forget that she died. I will never forget her. But yes, knowing the truth helps."

With the pad of his thumb, he brushed a tear off her cheek. "Here's another truth, Meg. I love you."

She looked him in the eye. "I love you, too. Always have. Always will."

He smiled. "Will you marry me? Again?"

Epilogue

The Montoyas were remarried two weeks later in a ceremony in the backyard of Sam and Claire Vernelli's house. The bride wore a simple cream-colored dress and the groom, who had threatened to wear cargo shorts, wore black dress pants, a blue shirt and a big smile. The police chaplain did the honors, keeping it short as requested by the groom. There wasn't a dry eye in the place when the happy couple, standing before a trellis of fresh flowers, pledged their love to one another.

There was cake and punch after the ceremony, which the bride promptly threw up. Afterward, her sort-of-new husband patted her hand and wiped her face with a cool cloth.

Claire Vernelli looked on with sympathy in her eyes and Sam handed Cruz a box of saltine crackers. Then Sam wrapped an arm protectively around Claire's slightly rounded stomach and pulled her close. He looked across the yard at his brother Jake, who had driven down for the weekend to help get the yard and house ready. He had one arm around Joanna, who was already starting to show with their second child and the other around his young daughter, who had slept through the ceremony.

"No more cake for you, Aunt Meg," said Jana, who'd done a bang-up job as flower girl. She danced around, twirling the ribbons on her dress, her white, patent-leather dress shoes sliding on the freshly mowed grass.

"At least not for another three months or so," said Cruz's mother, her brown eyes filled with happiness. "Welcome back," she said to her daughter-in-law and held her tight.

Cruz led his wife to a chair under a big shade tree. "Are you sure you feel up to the trip?"

"Yes. Definitely yes. I have a week off before I start my new job in Chicago."

"I still feel bad about your having to leave your job in San Antonio."

"Don't even think about it. I wanted to come back to Chicago. There are other hotels. There's only one you."

He kissed her. "I love you."

She smiled. "I know. Now, let's get going. We deserve that third honeymoon at Mackinaw Island. Are you packed?"

He nodded and tucked a piece of her short hair behind her ear. "Yep. Packed light. Didn't even bother pretending that I'd use the bike shorts."

* * * * *

LARGER-PRINT BOOKS!

GET 2 FREE LARGER-PRINT NOVELS PLUS
2 FREE GIFTS!

H HARLEQUIN®

INTRIGUE®

BREATHTAKING ROMANTIC SUSPENSE

YES! Please send me 2 FREE LARGER-PRINT Harlequin Intrigue® novels and my 2 FREE gifts (gifts are worth about $10). After receiving them, if I don't wish to receive any more books, I can return the shipping statement marked "cancel." If I don't cancel, I will receive 6 brand-new novels every month and be billed just $5.24 per book in the U.S. or $5.99 per book in Canada. That's a saving of at least 13% off the cover price! It's quite a bargain! Shipping and handling is just 50¢ per book in the U.S. and 75¢ per book in Canada.* I understand that accepting the 2 free books and gifts places me under no obligation to buy anything. I can always return a shipment and cancel at any time. Even if I never buy another book, the two free books and gifts are mine to keep forever.

199/399 HDN FVQ7

Name	(PLEASE PRINT)

Address		Apt. #

City	State/Prov.	Zip/Postal Code

Signature (if under 18, a parent or guardian must sign)

Mail to the **Harlequin® Reader Service:**
IN U.S.A.: P.O. Box 1867, Buffalo, NY 14240-1867
IN CANADA: P.O. Box 609, Fort Erie, Ontario L2A 5X3

Are you a subscriber to Harlequin Intrigue books
and want to receive the larger-print edition?
Call 1-800-873-8635 today or visit www.ReaderService.com.

* Terms and prices subject to change without notice. Prices do not include applicable taxes. Sales tax applicable in N.Y. Canadian residents will be charged applicable taxes. Offer not valid in Quebec. This offer is limited to one order per household. Not valid for current subscribers to Harlequin Intrigue Larger-Print books. All orders subject to credit approval. Credit or debit balances in a customer's account(s) may be offset by any other outstanding balance owed by or to the customer. Please allow 4 to 6 weeks for delivery. Offer available while quantities last.

Your Privacy—The Harlequin® Reader Service is committed to protecting your privacy. Our Privacy Policy is available online at www.ReaderService.com or upon request from the Harlequin Reader Service.

We make a portion of our mailing list available to reputable third parties that offer products we believe may interest you. If you prefer that we not exchange your name with third parties, or if you wish to clarify or modify your communication preferences, please visit us at www.ReaderService.com/consumerchoice or write to us at Harlequin Reader Service Preference Service, P.O. Box 9062, Buffalo, NY 14269. Include your complete name and address.

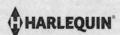